"Goodbye," said Henry and closed the door firmly......
Who ever kissed the trap goodbye?....

TO NAN, WITH LOVE.

# MURDER, ABSOLUTELY MURDER

## by
## Helen Cloutier

**WILDSIDE PRESS**

**www.wildsidepress.com**

# MURDER, ABSOLUTELY MURDER

# CHAPTER ONE

It was intuition rather than any one noise that brought Kari to sudden wakefulness.

Her bedside clock ticked softly underneath her new summer hat.

She lifted the rolled crown until the radium covered numbers of her traveler's clock were visible. The hands were sliding slowly toward seven o'clock.

She was aware of the missing smells, the warm, cloying odor of animal bodies, the smell of the barn from clothes hung in the back entry of their farm house. The smell of fresh egg coffee, boiling on the back of the stove. The smell of birch wood and pine needles, burning in the black kitchen range. The smell of plump loaves of baking bread and fat, raisin filled buns, awaiting their turn in the huge oven.

5

She was a long way from home, and her twitching nostrils drew in air freighted with an overtone of that unmistakable city-gas odor, the odor of diesel engines and burning fuel oil.

Escanaba. The realization was enough to animate Kari as she sat up and hugged her knees under her chin. At last. Escanaba. The roar of the diesel, switching carloads of iron ore from the ore-dock to number two yard, the short blasts of a lake freighter entering the harbor and signaling to the dock with sharp blasts on the ship's deep-throated horn, were typical Escanaba sounds. Escanaba, the busy shopping center of Michigan's Upper Peninsula.

At noon today, Rock would arrive by plane from Milwaukee. Tomorrow they would visit the city hall for their license, unless Rock still had the old one. Wednesday they would exchange their marriage vows.

Her heart beat thumpingly, with excitement. At twenty-three, she was ready for marriage, for Rock.

Rock Harris was a dermatologist, a skin specialist with a flourishing business in Milwaukee. He was becoming known for his cures for various skin and scalp diseases hitherto uncurable. They would return to Rock's quarters after the short honeymoon where Kari could redecorate and feminize the apartment.

Kari threw back the covers and stretched like a lazy, waking kitten. It would be fun to plan, to cook for Rock and to live in the city again, she thought.

Reaching for her gay corduroy high-heeled mules, and matching robe, she donned them and moved to the window. The hotel, named for one of the first thriving business men of the town, looked out over the soft blue of Little Bay de Noque. In the background, the huge, centipede-like boat churned skillfully to a stop beside the towering ore dock. Atop the trestle, the distant switch-engine looked tiny, dwarfed, as it pushed cars full of ore over the ore pockets. She watched, fascinated, when at a given signal from the switchman, the doorman opened the trap doors of a car and tripped the load into the pocket to be loaded into the squatting lake freighter below.

She turned away from the window and crossed to the dresser. With a few flourishes of her comb, the blonde hair fell into place. She moved back to the window, fascinated by the panorama before her.

Soon Rock would be here. Rock, as sturdy and reliable as his name. Tall, with a crew-cut thatch of dark hair and those startling, electric blue eyes. In his doctor's coat of white, she remembered how he'd looked when she'd last seen him three months ago.

He'd just returned from a trip to New York, where he'd been asked to speak before a group of skin specialists on his new formula.

After recall to active duty with the reserves and twenty-three months with the Far East command, he had returned with an inner excitement and several untried ideas. By the time he was discharged his excitement had become a festering cause. That had been a year ago.

Kari, laboratory technician, had met Rock while he was conducting experiments with the new formula at Millden Laboratories. It was love at first sight for both of them.

Then frantic word of the big fire had separated them Then the double funeral.

The muted sound of a bell brought Kari's thoughts back

7

to the present and she ran to the hat covered alarm clock.

"Darn! I thought I had that turned off," she stopped suddenly, hand suspended over the silent clock. Then she realized it was the telephone ringing.

Who would be calling her? She was a stranger here. It could only be Rock. He had registered for her by phone. He'd driven in early, probably rode all night just to surprise her.

"Yes?" her voice was eager, expectant.

A sharp intake of breath was audible from the other end of the phone. Then, the soft, velvety voice of a woman answered. The flesh on Kari's forearms raised in goose pimples. The voice was resonant, low.

"There must be some mistake," the voice was saying, "please excuse it." The click of the other phone preceded a long silence in which Kari replaced the phone in its cradle. Funny.

A moment later, as she was lifting her new hat from the clock, the shrill ring of the phone made her jump nervously.

"Hello!"

"Not again!" The same voice said. "Who is this? Is Rock there?"

Rock! How had anyone known where to call him? Was he in town? But he couldn't be, he'd have called. Her answer was slow and deliberate as she tried to keep the disturbed tremor from her voice.

"I expect him this morning. Shall I have him call you?" She kept her voice cool, impersonal.

"Who is this?" This time the question was insolent, impertinent.

Kari hesitated only an instant, then answered. "I'm Rock's fiancee, Kari Brent—who are you?"

The woman at the other end of the line groaned, a

muffled, animal-like sound, but a groan nevertheless. Then the click of the receiver as it rattled in place.

As Kari replaced the phone on the bedside table, her bewilderment was complete. What queer behavior, she thought. But soon Rock would be here. She would find peace and contentment at last, with his arms tightly around her. Nothing could matter for long. And in three days she would become Mrs. Rock Harris! She spoke the name softly as she slipped from her pajamas and into the needle spray shower.

A few minutes later, as she was putting the last bit of lipstick on with a lip-brush, a husky rap shook the hotel door.

Heavens, she thought, now what! She walked to the door.

"Rock!" Her squeal and the frantic dash into the young man's open arms was climaxed as he lifted her from the floor, her arms tight around his neck, and kissed her tenderly. She buried her face in the tweed shoulder, which held the faint, pleasant odor of tobacco and old spice.

"My darling," Rock held her away from him now, his blue eyes scanning her face as if to make sure it was not a dream, that it was really she. He frowned slightly, his head tilted to one side, the professional gesture she remembered so well.

"A bit on the pale side," he grinned at her, "but I think you'll live."

She snuggled against him again, wondering why his remark made her tremble. "Silly," she rubbed his closely shaven cheek with her snub nose, "now that you're here I'll live forever."

"That's my girl," he ran his fingers through the back

9

of the thick mane of blonde hair. "I'd almost wondered whether I'd had hallucinations, dreamed you up in one of my more brilliant moments," he laughed as she lifted her soft lips for another kiss. A brief pause while he supplied the demand, then, "Almost convinced myself you were only a test tube mirage. But darling," his voice grew a little strained, "I'm no bargain, no angel. Never have been. You know so little about me. I made one mistake—" his words were almost inaudible. "But I know I can make you happy." It was almost a vow, the way he said it.

Kari raised her brown eyes to his, her finger tips aganist his lips. "Hush, Rock. Never even think of this being anything but right. You're the only thing worth while I've left in this whole world."

"I hope you're right, baby. I only hope you're right." He moved to the one deep chair in the room. "And before you can be sure, there are things I must explain. Things you'll have to know, to face."

"Not now, darling. Maybe sometime, but not now." Kari pressed her lips tight against his and for a long moment they were lost in each other.

The jangling of the telephone startled and separated them. "No calls now," Rock warned.

"Maybe you'd better answer. Someone called for you just before you came. A woman, with a voice like an angel." Kari moved away then.

Rock looked at her. The expression on his face was one she'd never seen before. He reached for the phone slowly, cautiously.

"Yes?" His one word seemed long, drawn out as if he hated to end it, as if he knew what was coming.

10

Rock was saying. "But how did you know—?" He paused, "no. I suppose so."

Kari could hear the soft voice now, as Rock held the receiver away from his ear and looked at it in a dazed sort of stupor. He was paying no attention to what the voice was saying.

Instinctively Kari took the receiver from Rock's hand. An audible click sounded as she grasped it and she knew the voice was gone.

How could anyone, anything, make him look like that? With death around him in Korea he could never have looked more angry than he did now. His voice rasped with a throb she had never before heard and his eyes glinted.

"They told her at the office I'd be here. I'll have to leave you for a little while. I'm sorry, darling." He clasped her to him as if to reassure himself she was still here, still his girl. "I'll make it up to you, I promise!" he murmured.

"Of course." She pressed her face hard into the tweed shoulder again. She could feel the thumping beat of his heart against her temple and she knew, without asking, this was his mistake, the thing about which he must talk.

"Everything will be all right, Rock. No matter what has happened or what could happen, remember that. You and me, always!"

He shook his head, the dazed look still in his eyes but the fear was gone. It had been a momentary thing, fleeting, but unmistakable. In its place was a sort of rage.

"It might as well be now. Before we're married," he said. "I've been a coward. Now you'll have to suffer. Perhaps we should have waited."

His arms tightened around her again, pressed her close, hurting, as if to protect her from the unknown.

11

"Don't worry." Kari answered. "Nothing can hurt us, Rock. We have each other." As she spoke she couldn't help thinking, "his mind is on something—the voice I'm sure. Whatever it is, means trouble. But I don't care. It can't touch me—us! It won't let it! This mistake he talks of is past!

# CHAPTER TWO

"Is it true that Mrs. Donald Jeffries is going to sue you, Mrs. Norton?"

"Would you care to give us a statement? Maybe a picture?"

The reporters from the two local papers stood waiting for a reply, the press photographers with camera poised, ready. They had been asking questions for the past hour.

MacAllister Norton was growing impatient, the pile of cigarettes in the ash tray at her elbow threatened to overflow at any moment. She sat, huddled in the corner of an overstuffed fan chair, looking like a small child being scolded. A lock of flaming red hair fell over her broad forehead, almost touching the black brows. The men clustered around her, some sitting, some squatting on their haunches trying to bring themselves down to her level. They were admiring her beauty. And she did look childish as she watched them with carefully guarded eyes. She must not display her temper, everything must go smoothly. She exuded charm and perhaps a bit of fear with her blue eyes wide, moving from one face to another. She knew they were thinking how impossible it was to think her of doing anything such as Mrs. Jeffries was accusing her of.

She knew she could control the press, as least those in the room now. They were pitying her, she knew it, she could feel it in their admiring glances, their questions. Under her calm exterior, she laughed cynically at the fools.

"What does your husband think of this, Mrs. Norton? Have you hired any other lawyer? And your son, he's in fourth, isn't he?"

MacAllister squirmed to a more comfortable position, her foot was going to sleep. She wished they'd leave. She chose her answers carefully.

"Mr. Norton was upset, naturally. But we don't believe we'll need any other lawyer. Stan is very competent. I'm sure that Mrs. Jeffries is being overly hysterical, that she will withdraw the case. And Paul, of course modern children are much more calm than their parents in most cases, don't you think?

And Benjamin Florietto, the long-legged, black-haired man, hair stylist for the MacAllister Style Clinic was glad when the reporters had gone. He walked with the men to the door. He was evidently surprised that MacAllister had continued calm when question after question was hurled at her. He returned to her side.

MacAllister stretched and slid gracefully from the big chair.

14

"Imbeciles! Morons! As if Dolly Jeffries could hurt me *or* my business. You know what's itching her, don't you Bengy? Her smile was malicious, calculated.

"If you're insinuating anything, I fail to see the humor in it."

"Because you don't want to Bengy, dear." Her soft insidious tone held hint of threat. "I know that Dotty has always been jealous of me—ever since I took Stan away from her. She's tried before, to get a hold on him. I know that too! Now she'd like to ruin my business—get at him that way."

Her eyes snapped as she raised them to look into his face. The expression had changed. He was used to scenes and evidently tired of them. He looked at her and it was almost pity she read in his eyes. She knew she could wind him around her finger.

"But of course she won't. Stan will see to that," MacAllister slid her hands down the sides of her hips and thighs appraisingly. A smile twitched at the corners of her lips.

"Awfully sure of yourself, aren't you, Mac?" Bengy stood watching her. "Remember, back in beauty school. If I hadn't pulled you through some of those tests, baby—"

"Don't remind me."

His grin came easy. "I won't. You'll remind yourself. But don't forget, without me, you'd never have passed the State Board. I pounded those answers into your head."

"And never let me forget it!"

"You've been too willing to try. But I won't let you." Bengy smiled, but not at MacAllister. It was a tight, private grin and the next words were only for himself, "and all you wanted was a small, successful business that we could both live contentedly on, a home of our own—together. When I think of these last years I'm almost

15

sorry I ever helped you. I'm ashamed of what it's developed into."

She opened her blue eyes wide and pushed the fiery locks back from her forehead, antagonizing him. "And if you had it to do over again, Bengy?" her eyes were half closed now, demandnig.

His eyes never left her face. He gazed as one transfixed.

"You are in my blood, MacAllister, my life. I've been a part of your growth. Your ambitions have been my ambitions, your problems my problems, your hates and loves, my hates and loves. I know you better than you know yourself."

Only her eyelids twitched as Bengy spoke, but he obviously could feel the tension between them as she answered, her voice a muted purr, "Money—yes! I love it, I'll have it too—and lots of it! They'll never get another chance to look over their noses at me. Never!"

"Mac, Mac—" Bengy sighed. "First it was only a little. But a little was not enough. It must be more, more, more! When will the saturation point come, Mac, when? And, when it does come, if ever, will you be able to sit back and relax? You've walked a long road."

"I'll relax some day. Of course tomorrow, I'll have more, more money, more prestige, more pull. Rock will see to that."

"Rock!"

Her black lashes swept down, muting the blue challenge of her eyes. She was intense. She had been saving Rock as a surprise.

"Rock's in town. I called Milwaukee."

Bengy ran his tongue over his thin lips stretched tight across his white teeth. "At last. I knew you'd manage it some way. Does it give you pleasure to dig into the past? Wasn't one knock-down, drag-out fiasco enough?"

"I couldn't use him then. Now, Doctor Harris can swing this whole mess in my favor! Who will try to dispute the word of a famous specialist?"

"Yes. I can see the headlines. Prominent Milwaukee doctor convinces local authorities—"

MacAllister lifted the curtains to the blue eyes again. "Um-hum."

"Could be that you married the wrong fellow?" Bengy frowned. "Nice, prominent Doctor now. When he gives his report, you'll be cleared. In fact it will boost your business. And if he won't play?"

"He'll play."

"That, of course, remains to be seen. His words will be expert and he won't perjure, even for you. He's a man now, Mac. Doctor Rock Harris, Dermatologist. He knows the answers. You can't twist him around your finger."

MacAllister slid her hands down over her slim hips in a feline gesture. "One can always try—. He'll be over later."

"You hope!"

She grinned now. It was a crafty, sly grin, eyes half lidded, menacing. "I know. He'll be here."

# CHAPTER THREE

The Greyhound bus with 'Milwaukee' on its forehead roared around the curve. Its last rest-stop completed and only the remaining tens of miles to its destination. The driver looked into his mirror again. He watched the salesman letting his body lurch against the red headed teenager from the Escanaba stop. What a shape, what a pair of—. She had given him a flash of blue eyes when her suitcase had banged him below the beltline as she turned away when he had suggested that she could have the seat behind him so she wouldn't be lonesome. When he had picked up his tickets from the floor, she was sitting well down the aisle. The sales-type fellow hadn't wasted any time.

The driver could have told her that the salesman never did waste his time on any of the eight or nine occasions he'd seen him get off in Milwaukee and head for the

Peyton Hotel across the street from the terminal—with a chick, sixteen to sixty, on his arm. Well, not sixty, but not far away from that. He had only wanted to keep this eighteen-year older from that tail-happy wolf.

"So, I can get your course-cost five hundred dollars off as a scholarship winner from Escanaba—you're in my territory," the salesman drooled. Her pointed breast punched his forearm again. It was delightful, the way she understood him. That he had to change the name of the scholarship winner on his report, switch the vote-count report from twelve of his stops to Escanaba. That his boss would get a quart of Black Label.

All that to make MacAllister Heminger the Beauty Aids Line's $500 scholarship winner to the Lewis School of Beauty Culture.

"You're so very sweet to me—Henry. I'm so surprised—and I'll be so grateful." MacAllister said caressingly, her breast rubbing.

"I'll register you at my hotel—it's a block from the school and you'll save carfare," Henry said as the driver brought the bus to a final stop in the terminal.

MacAllister's blue eye winked once as she followed Henry out of the bus. The driver's eyes widened as he stared after them. That little teenage redhead had the bus ride planned from the start. He watched them cross the street and go into the Peyton Hotel . . .

"Now, Henry—I'm going back to my room. You've had your money's worth."

"Money's worth—hey Mac?" Henry sat up in bed. He watched the beautiful redhead cupping her wonderful breasts into the filmy confinement of the brassiere.

"The scholarship to the Lewis School, Henry." said

MacAllister. She smiled sweetly, her blue eyes were icy. "Your report, the vote-count report, the quart of Black Label—for Mr. Bazely."

"Black Label—for Mr. Bazely?"

"I'll be at Lewis School of Beauty Culture, tomorrow morning, to pick up my scholarship or Mr. Walter Bazely will know why, or Mrs. Henry Lundgren will know why"

"And I'll know why," Henry pulled the covers over his head groaning. He had less than twenty hours to perform what had taken seconds to propose . . .

MacAllister met Henry in the Lewis School building. He had performed life a wolf caught in a trap. It had taken a case of Black Label and a gallon of sweat, but the little wolf-trapping redhead was officially the Beauty Aids Line's winner from Escanaba—and so he told the registrar.

"I'll always be grateful for the effort you made for me, Henry." said Mac. They were outside the building. She squeezed his arm and rubbed as before but Henry's mind was on other things.

"I'll have to call my wife," said Henry worriedly. He knew there was going to be hell to pay when he got home. He always got home on Friday night—here it was Saturday.

"Mrs. Lundgren called, while you were out this morning," said Mac smiling at Henry's widening eyes. "Mr. Bazely's secretary had told her where you were. I told her I was Alice Gordon, in Beauty Aids public relations department and was helping you get the scholarship winner decided."

"You know Alice Gordon too?" Henry muttered. They went into the hotel. Henry felt that never in his life, had he been so trapped. He didn't even snarl when Mac-

Allister told the desk clerk that Beauty Aids was taking care of her rent.

"For one month," Henry whispered. Mac looked at him and smiled, she was generous in victory.

"For one month," she told the clerk. They went upstairs to the room. Henry silently got his suitcase out of the closet and opened the room door to leave this trap.

"Aren't you going to kiss me goodbye, Henry?" said Mac, her long, sweet teenage legs were crossed at her slim ankles as she lay on the bed. Her blue eyes looked at him warmly.

"Goodbye," said Henry and closed the door firmly . . . Who ever kissed the trap goodbye? . . .

MacAllister was in the swing of things by the end of her first week in school. There was a difference between this school and the high school back home, and not just the months that had gone by since she graduated.

For one thing, there were fifty girls for every boy—not that she had ever worried about competing with any girl for any boy. The girls were all sizes, shapes and, ages— from sixteen on up. Some were even good looking. The boys were also good looking, in fact, all of them were good looking.

For another thing, this school was concerned with one subject and only one subject—how to make a woman's head beautiful. Not breasts or buttocks or thighs—just her head. And all the girls and boys concentrated on learning how to make that head beautiful—because they'd paid out money they had earned by working for it.

The big difference, MacAllister found, was that her femininity, her sexual invitation, or even the pressure of a pointed breast, had little or no effect on the boys. That was the big difference. These boys had some girl ingre-

21

dient in their makeup, and the more girl ingredient, the less MacAllister's ability to attract. The boys, most of them, weren't queer—they just had more girl in them.

When Mac found that out, she philosophically adjusted to the conditions and used her brains harder than she had ever done before in her eighteen years to learn the basic fundamentals of the beauty business, which would be her springboard to fame and wealth and a place in society that was denied her; she had been raised on the wrong side of the tracks in Escanaba . . .

"Wait for me, Mac, I'll buy your supper."

MacAllister turned back toward the voice from her rear. Classes were over this first day of the second week at Lewis.

The voice belonged to one of the three boys in her class, Benjamin Florietto, tall, slim, dark eyed, and dark haired. He towered almost six feet. She waited for him curiously. He had gone to barber college and had been a barber for six months but had decided to enroll in Lewis to learn hair styling. She remembered him telling some of the boys how much he had disliked having to be so close to one strange man after another while he cut their hair. She had smiled at that in surprise. It could be that he even liked girls.

"I live at the Peyton too," Benjamin told Mac. They had been to a drive-in hamburger stand in his shabby convertible. Mac had found that he'd been a farm boy. His parents had been killed at a railroad crossing. He sold the farm and had come to Milwaukee to learn barbering, and now to learn hair styling.

"I heard that you don't like strange men," Mac was mischievous.

"Only when they nuzzle me when I'm cutting their hair."

"How are you going to feel when the girls start nudging you when you're styling their hair?"

Benjamin laughed, "I think I'll like it—I haven't cut any girl's hair yet—next week maybe." They walked across the hotel lobby to the elevator.

"Want to come up with me, Bengy?" MacAllister was speculative.

"Bengy?" Benjamin said and looked down into her sparkling eyes and blushed. "Sure, Mac. I live on the same floor—"

Sure he lived on her floor—since yesterday, when he found out where she was staying. The desk clerk had leered when he asked if a Miss MacAllister Heminger was registered there. And did he want his room on the same floor—maybe the room next to it? It could be arranged—if . . .

The if was five bucks extra, and Benjamin Florietto was next door and a wall away from losing his cherry— as the fellows back home called it.

"Open it." Mac handed him the key. Benjamin's fingers trembled as he opened the door and her flaming red, smoky smelling hair brushed lightly under his chin.

She switched on the bed lamp after putting her books on the dresser. The room was like his. A single bed, bed lamp, a small table beside the bed, a wooden chair, an armchair and an iron floor lamp near the window. The other door led to the bathroom that his room shared with hers. There were locks on both sides of the doors and he guessed that you were supposed to lock the other door when you wanted to use the bathroom and unlock it afterwards, and vice versa.

"Let me take your coat, Bengy," Mac said and her blue eyes were lazy. She reached up to unbutton his top coat. He looked down at her and blushed. She hung his coat in the small cabinet beside the room door and then took off her black gabardine all-weather coat and hung it beside his. Bengy watched the swelling of her breasts as she stretched and wet his lips. He had wanted a woman, for the first time in his twenty years of life, when he first saw her in his class. Now he was alone with her, in a room, a bedroom. Alone with her.

"Hey, Bengy—the cat's got your tongue" said Mac openly laughing at him. She reached into the cabinet and pulled out a thin blue robe.

He swallowed hard and to his surprise heard himself saying: "I want to make love to you, Mac, I want to make love—but I don't know how—"

"You do?" Mac was smiling at him. She didn't seem to be offended. He took a shy step toward her. She held up a finger.

"Wait, Bengy, I want to be in something more comfortable first—" Mac went to the bathroom door, "It's locked —hell . . . I wonder who's next door."

"Me." Bengy was filled with a strange excitement. She had said to wait while she had gotten herself more comfortable—she hadn't become angry.

"I was wondering when you were going to tell me that you had moved in next door," Mac was laughing, peals of husky golden laughter that flooded him with her warmth. "The clerk told me this morning. Now will you please go to your room—and unlock the door?" She pushed him gently toward the hall door . . .

# CHAPTER FOUR

It was mid-day. The small assemblage had been listening to preliminary council and various counter-talk between several of the local authorities. The closed session had been set for nine-thirty. It was now almost twelve. Dottie Jeffries sat nervously whispering with a tall, pale young man near an open window. They were absorbed in what the other was saying. No one noticed nor paid any attention, other than a brief, glance, to the dark haired, hatless young man in oxford grey flannel jacket and gray flannel slacks who stepped quietly inside the door and seated himself.

One exception, Dr. Lewis Ford, local physician-surgeon, slipped unobtrusively from his chair nearby and extended a welcome hand.

"Rock—hello there."

"Nice to see you again, Lew," Rock answered.

"You in this?" Dr. Ford lifted an eyebrow in query.

"I'm not sure. I have more important things on my mind at present."

Dr. Ford's expression was bland. "Yes?"

"I can't be tied up here now with any of this petty, small town squabbling." He patted his coat pocket. "I've a license and a date with the preacher. My girl and I—. You certainly have someone else on your staff. Why me?"

"There's more here than meets the eye, Rock. There have been threats—unsigned letters—one of my men is in the convalescent ward."

"Coincidence, Lew. That has no bearing."

"Perhaps. But my man says it's more than that."

"Phooey. Small town stuff. Look, Lew, remember me?" He stopped for a moment. 'I know Escanaba! I lived here!"

"All the more reason for you to help out, Rock. You can see the truth," Dr. Ford spoke quietly, "and it will take someone who knows things, underneath the surface!" He paused, then plunged into direct attack. "Things about Stan. About MacAllister!"

"I can't. Not about Stan. He was my friend you know. I won't pry into his affairs."

"All right. So you don't pry. So you just call it as you see it, as Doctor Rock Harris, sees it. You know, Stan's a good friend of mine too. He's the one who asked me to persuade you to specialize."

"But what's all this rumor about scalp burning? Where does that bring Stan into the picture? Why the ruckus in the first place?"

Rock's eyes sparked dangerously as they met Dr. Ford's expressionless ones. "That's only part of the story. The rest is undercover, money-grabbing. Black-mail I believe it's called. And it's not new. It's been going on for some time."

"But Stan wouldn't—"

"I can't believe it either. And right now he needs you on his side, but he won't ask you."

Rock ran his fingers around the edge of his collar. His wry smile erased the frown that had begun to form on his high forehead. "There are other doctors here who could examine that burn."

"Yes, if that's all there is to it."

"Let's quit the double-talk, Doc," Rock said. "It's MacAllister who has you hog-tied."

Dr. Ford nodded.

"Are you sure?"

Yes. I'm certain. She's gone crazy the last few months over money. When it gets that bad, it gets out of control. It's no joke, Rock. Stan is on the edge of a collapse. This has to stop, and right now—before something worse happens! She's developed a snob complex."

Rock's face was stern, lined now. "She hasn't developed it, she's always had it."

"Shhh—" The doctor cautioned Rock. "She's getting up to say something—"

Rock stiffened. The back hair on his neck stood straight out as a chill flashed over him. He turned slowly, his eyes on a vacant spot mid-air, just over his knees. He didn't need to look at her. He could see her, without looking. A petite red-head, a muffled volcano, always on the verge of instantaneous explosion. Then she spoke. That's what really got him.

"Of course, this is all perfectly ridiculous. You know," she began in a soft, velvet voice, "not only ridiculous but terribly unfair and utterly silly." Her voice broke and she gulped childishly before she continued. "You all

27

know me, have known me for years. Dottie's imagination
has been working overtime. As for the burns, yes, there
was a very small one and of no consequence. We treated
it once in the shop and it is completely healed. In fact
it was healed the second day." She looked around carefully at the assembled group and her eyes hesitated
briefly as they flicked over Rock.

His eyes were still on the vacant spot. He shivered
without knowing why, except perhaps the velvet voice
could still stir him to depths, as it had when they'd
first met.

She continued to talk, explaining each detail leading
up to the accidental burn. Rock listened, not to the words,
but to that haunting throaty quality fo her voice. She
knew how to use it, how to make each one listening feel
that she was speaking for him alone. It was almost
hypnotic in its power to create the atmosphere of sincere
sympathy.

A harsh, grating snort of derision broke the spell as
Dottie moved her chair noisily across the floor to sit
closer to her attorney. The listeners relaxed again; obviously the illusion was broken. Dottie's loud whispers
and giggling continued, and began to be echoed from
several others. When MacAllister heard this her voice
dropped deeper, softer, and Rock could feel the seething
turmoil of unleashed vitriol in each spoken word.

He knew now that he must participate, must watch
and do what he could either way. He felt himself swayed
to MacAllister's support, as others in the room were
swayed. No matter what the past had held between them,
he knew he believed her, even against his better judg-
ment. Her voice, purring softly, still battered him relent-
lessly.

What she had said, he knew not. Words had flowed gently, evenly and he'd not heard. It was Dottie's giggling and raucous remarks that had alienated her in the minds of the neutrals. But her council had squelched it in time.

Bengy Florietto had moved unobtrusively to a chair at Rock's side. "Rock," he said, "with that voice she could almost make the devil knock on the pearly gates. If she only knew the punch it carries—. She's dangerous."

"She certainly is, believe me!" Rock answered as he stood abruptly, as if unwilling to discuss MacAllister with anyone. He nodded briefly at Bengy and walked to the door. He turned and his eyes were drawn to MacAllister's with the pull of magnet to steel. She was watching him and the sun made a halo of red around her face as it streamed through the windows at her back. Her eyes mocked him with that half-lidded look he knew so well. She smiled at him.

Rock shut the door firmly from the outside and went back to Kari, to the hotel. As he held her warm body close, with her arms around his neck, he was no longer afraid. He no longer could hear the voice with its malevolent urge. Kari's lips were soft and fresh and cool against his.

He would give a statement. It would release him. Kari would understand, perhaps better than he. It would finish things definitely. Bengy obviously knew her too, knew how dangerous she was. But he'd call Stan first, he was still his friend, even though he was MacAllister's husband.

His lips found Kari's again and he lost himself for a moment. He could feel the thudding of her heart. He buried his face in the thick blonde mane. "I'll have to do this, Kari, Maybe you'd better go back home till it's over. It won't take long."

Kari turned her face up to his. "Rock, darling, I'm never going back. I want to be here, with you. Oh, Rock, I love you so much, I wonder if you realize—. I can't leave you."

Of course she wouldn't go. He'd known it before he spoke but he wanted to hear it from her lips. She was his girl, all the way. He needed her more than she knew. He couldn't make her go and wouldn't have if he could. But he tried again, not believing what he said, "This may prove to be a nasty business—"

"Of course, darling," Kari chuckled, "so I can play it safe and run back to the farm I no longer have. I'm staying."

It was final and he was glad. Together the undercurrent of this nasty little business would seem nothing. They were in love. His arms pressed her to him again.

Could he let her stay? Then his answer came, muffled in the thick fluff of her hair as his lips caressed her temple, "Good."

He could protect her. There's be no real danger to Kari from any barbs thrust by MacAllister.

MacAllister. The pulse in his throat seemed to choke him. He chilled at the thought of her, and what had been.

# CHAPTER FIVE

She was on the table when Rock came on emergency duty, her dark lashes resting on her cheek. Her beautiful red hair against the white of her uniform matched the red blood splashes on her skirt. He thought she was a nurse until he saw the flesh colored stockings. She must be a technician in a laboratory or a beautician. Another girl lay on the second table and Len Fallon was working on her wrists with needle and catgut. A tall, slim, dark young man in a white smock leaned against the wall smoking a cigarette.

"What does the redhead need?" Rock asked Len.

"I think you could kiss her—that would wake her up," said Len over his shoulder. "She wore herself out wrestling with this gal over the razor blade—I told her to lay down and rest."

31

Rock walked over to the other table. He looked down at the redhead. She was really asleep. He studied her perfect face. The skin was absolutely flawless, a creamy golden tone with faint shades of rose. Skin tones were beginning to lead him deeper into the mysteries of skin allergies, the conditions that created blemishes on the human skin. The treatment was a vast field in which he was going to specialize. Her lips were full without being too full, almost like ripe fruit. There was something familiar about her.

Enormous blue eyes opened and stared into his, a few inches above hers. Her lips parted and she smiled lazily, her head moved the few inches and Rock felt the electri-like shock of pleasure from the soft wamth of her mouth against his. Her arms came around his neck and brought her up with him as he straightened.

"Doctor Rock Harris, I presume," MacAllister said calmly as she released him and sat up on the table. Rock could almost feel Len smiling behind him. He looked over his shoulder—he was.

"We're both from Escanaba, Rock—you used to skate with me sometimes," MacAllister said. Her sitting position now allowed the fullness of her breasts to thrust against the white nylon of her uniform.

"I remember, I remember," Rock heard himself saying. This was the first time he had ever kissed anyone in the hospital. It was almost six years since he'd left Escanaba— and he didn't remember this gorgeous creature at all, even if she did look familiar. Then his memory clicked.

MacAllister Heminger. Stan had sent him a snapshot of her and her name had been whispered in Escanaba while he was away at school. The whispered name that sometimes became a whistle . . .

"What's going on—class reunion? The old man'll be down here any minute now," warned Len. The girl with

the slashed wrists tried to sit up and he shook his head
at her to stay down.

"Did you bring her in?" Rock asked as he made out the
report.

"Yes, Bengy Florietto and I—we live on the same floor
at the Peyton. We heard groans and found her kneeling
at the bath tub," Mac said, as she swung her long slim
legs down to the emergency room tile floor. She knew
Rock was watching her over his report form as she lifted
her skirt above her knees to check the splashes of blood.
It was a personal look—not professional.

"I'm at the Lewis school for three more weeks—and in
room 906 at the Peyton—if you'd like to come over and talk
about Escanaba . . ." Mac said quickly, before she went out
of the room. The tall, dark fellow waited for her silently.

Rock smiled and nodded his head, "First chance I get,
Mac."

"Dr. Kildare you are wanted in surgery—" Len said
mockingly. Rock smiled at Len and helped him with the
girl until the police arrived with two car-accident victims
. . . Room 906 at the Peyton . . .

"Come on in, Rock." He opened the door with 906 on it
and entered. MacAllister was leaning toward a mirror on
the wall above a chest of drawers, her hand held a tiny
brush that she used to stroke her eyelashes. He saw her red
lips, smiling at him and puckering up in a kiss, in the mirror. She wore only the sheerest of black panties. The in-
credible richness of her breasts swung gently with the
movement of her arm.

Rock felt a shock of pleasure and had to lean back
against the closed door for support. She put the small
brush down and turned to face him, her sparkling blue

eyes were glowing but there was a deliberate calmness in her face and movement. He saw a bottle of champagne in an ice bucket beside the bed and two glasses on the small table.

"Aren't you going to wish me a happy ninteenth birthday?" Mac came toward him slowly, her arms held out, breasts swaying.

He felt his tongue thickening and his breath becoming shallow, and he could only manage to whisper, "Happy birthday." Yesterday, he had kissed her on the emergency room table; today he was going to make love to her on her bed . . .

"I'm going to open a Beauty Salon with Mac, next week." said Bengy quietly. His face had a sterness that Rock had not seen the various times that Bengy had been around MacAllister when he'd come over from the hospital. The weeks had flown.

"Where, in Milwaukee?" Rock asked politely. They were in the Peyton lobby. Bengy had been waiting for him. Mac had told him about Bengy—how helpful and useful he was at school.

"He keeps all the wolves off . . ." Mac said.

"How did I get by him?" Rock asked. She had come close and snuggled in his arms.

"I wanted you, Rock—and I get what I want."

"No, Mac wants to go back to Escanaba," Bengy said. He looked at Rock steadily, "I love MacAllister, I'd marry her if she'd have me—she won't, but I'll always be near her."

"Okay, Bengy—I love her too. But I can't marry her either—I've got three more years to go before I can support a wife and children—"

The background buzzing that had been going on while

they were talking broke into a roar. Rock and Bengy turned to the group of people around the radio.

"The Japs bombed Pearl Harbor!"

# CHAPTER SIX

Stan hung the receiver back in its cradle. Rock, good old Rock, was here. He rubbed his damp forehead with a shaking hand. He ached with weariness. He knew his doctor would put him to bed if he called him, would tell him he'd gone against orders, to relax, let down more, take it easy.

He'd stop at the hotel to see Rock, who'd been his friend so long ago.

The intercom buzzed. His secretary's voice came through metallically, unnatural, when he flipped the switch and said, "Yes?"

"Reporters from the Milwaukee Express are here to see you, Mr. Norton."

"Come here a moment first, Miss McCormick."

A moment later he explained to the bewildered girl.

"Have them wait fifteen minutes, then tell them I've gone. I'll leave by the other door."

"Yes, Mr. Norton." She looked back over her shoulder at him as she left.

He grabbed his hat and opened the other door cautiously. Alone in the hall, he walked down one floor and picked up the elevator from there. His shoulders had a stoop and he tried to straighten when he saw his reflection in the elevator mirror. Of late the burden of MacAllister's problems had bent them more than a little. He remembered pre-MacAllister days—days of fun.

He trudged wearily along the sidewalk of Ludington street, hardly lifting his feet enough to clear the warmness of it. Past Joe's Coffee Cup where once he'd been welcome, past Greenfields Real Estate office where he used to chat with Pat Greenfield and his two lovely daughters. He dared not even look, he couldn't face the varying expressions he found in them. They were all, more or less, victims of MacAllister's climb to money, her bid for "more money than you can shake a stick at."

Past the banks, the Chevrolet garage, the Daily Press building, with its humming behive of activity. On, on, down Ludington past the fresh-bread smells of the bakery, the heavy cloying odor of the hide house, past the Delta Hardware.

He should have stopped for his car, but he'd been aware of reporters lurking in the parking lot. It was good to walk again, he'd become too dependent on cabs, his car. His step grew quicker, his stride longer. He would soon see Rock. He walked more erect, his brown eyes squinting against the bright glare of afternoon sun against the pavement.

At the hotel door he stopped, faced the bay and watched, for a moment, the activity on number-six ore dock. Then he entered and took the elevator to the third floor. Rock had said room 317.

He rapped twice.

The door opened cautiously and a girl, blonde, brown-eyed and beautiful, stood facing him.

"Hello."

He liked her manner immediately. "Have I made a mistake? Isn't this Dr. Rock Harris' room?"

"Yes. I'm waiting for him. I'm Kari Brent, Rock's fiancee."

Stan couldn't help stammering. "I — I'm surprised — pleasantly though! Indeed, pleasantly!" His voice was emphatic. He held out his hand. "I'm Stan Norton."

"Of course. I should have known. Come in, please." Kari's hand clasped his warmly and she drew him across the threshold. "Rock should be back here any minute." She turned brown eyes up to brown eyes. "Rock's best friend—"

"I hope so," he answered.

Kari sensed the tenseness, the hesitation as he answered. She continued to hold his hand and led him to the easy chair by the window, overlooking Bay de Noque, giving him time to calm his nerves.

"Rock should be back any minute," she repeated gently, "he's very anxious to see you."

Relief flooded over Stan as he leaned back in the chair and stared out of the window. This girl of Rock's was talking to him like a child, and for a moment he listened thankfully. He sighed heavily and relaxed.

So this is Rock's girl. But if Mac has arranged for Rock to talk for her, what can this child do against her? She hasn't a chance against MacAllister, not a ghost! Poor Rock, poor Kari!

Kari leaned against the wide, winged window and stared out across the water. The silence was friendly between them. Then she turned slightly to face him.

"Tell me about Rock, Mr. Norton?" Her question was almost a plea.

Stan smiled a little at the eager face and talked of his friend. How much did she know of MacAllister and Rock?

In the silence, when he paused to remember more for her, Kari looked at him. "And then you and Rock quarreled."

Stan nodded, not trusting his voice.

"Rock told me he flew off his rocker."

His memory turned back to the quarrel and he knew how typical it was that Rock assume the blame.

"I guess we were both a little foolish. It wasn't Rock's fault. We were both involved and—well," he hesitated trying to find words, "I guess the truth was pretty rugged to understand, especially as Rock was inexperienced, young."

"It's forgotten now, Stan, whatever it was." Kari's face was glowing, her brown eyes big, luminous.

The chair grated harshly as he flung himself from it. "By all that's good and holy and if you want to marry Rock, get him out of Escanaba. Before it's too late.

Kari looked startled for only an instant. Somehow she seemed to understand. "And if he won't go?"

"I'll help you. You must leave. I'll see to it. Just tell him I'm leaving the case. He'll understand."

He knew he'd have to help. MacAllister would never let another woman have him, he'd once belonged to her.

"It's getting late. Have Rock call me. I'll be at home."

Stan hated to do what he knew he must do. His steps dragged as he walked down Ludington street, past the point and down Lake Shore Drive. Shade trees formed a dome-like tent of coolness as the south breeze off the Lake tossed them gently overhead. Two blocks, three blocks, then their home. Big, pretentious, a monstrosity of the old lumbering-era when Escanaba boomed and fortunes were made in logs and liquor, when lumber-jacks and ladies drank in separate rooms.

He was tired. As he hung his hat in the hall closet he realized just how tired he was. If only he could put this off. But it had to be done now. Now or never. He knew Mac would be dressing. He didn't hurry up the long, open stairway.

MacAllister heard him at the doorway to her room. She sat brushing her fiery red hair in front of the huge mirror of her dressing table. "We'll be late at the club dinner if you don't hurry," she purred, her voice soft.

He shuddered slightly and knew it was fear, "I'm staying home."

Her blue eyes flashed at his in the mirror. He could feel them. She continued to brush.

"Certainly you're going. We're expected." The soft words were like manacles.

"Expected! So what!" His words were bitter.

"So we are going. Get dressed." The throaty sound of her voice sickened him. "After today, nothing can stop us. Stan Norton, lawyer, and MacAllister, his lovely wife. Nothing can touch us now."

"Touch you, don't you mean, Mac?"

Her eyes flicked dangerously and she pursed her red lips into a tight line.

He found, too late, that he'd made his grave mistake. It was not easy to believe of her, that so much evil, malice and hatred could be concealed in the tiny frame. Her fiery hair curled gently around her peach-complexioned face, a sprinkling of pale freckles splashed over the bridge

**40**

of her nose, venetian-blue eyes framed in long black lashes were set carefully under a low, wide brow.

If only he could break that terrible spell, that of trusting her, believing her. But, as with all her victims, he too, was powerless against her magnetism.

She continued to watch him, as a cat watches a mouse.

Stan knew that behind her calm exterior raced a razor-sharp mind. He knew that she had already jumped six steps ahead of him. That she would continue on the same path as inexortable as a robot, with one end in view. She uncurled from the huge padded stool and slipped the sheathlike gown of gold faille over her head.

He waited for her next words, and she played for time. She knew the art of suspense and held her reply in abeyance. Then he repeated, "I'm staying home, Mac. Go if you wish. However, I'll not represent you in whatever hocus-pocus you're cooking up. I'm through."

"You're through?"

He made no answer.

She repeated softly, "You're not representing me?"

Stan shook his head. "No, Mac. This is your baby. You bore it! You worked for the devil, now have his offspring. I can't, I won't be a part of it."

"You're in it now! You can't back out!"

"I was a fool!" he said. "You had me buffaloed for a while. I didn't think you'd actually go through with it. When I saw you were serious, I tried to stop you. Stopping you is like trying to stop a bolt of lightning. But I'm through, Mac. All done. Beauty Shop squabbles I can fight and forget. Blackmail! — That's out. I've had it."

"But you said —"

"Maybe I did say I'd see what I could do. But blackmail! And my own, personal friends! Your conniving and dirty dealing."

41

"Coward!"

"Maybe. But one dirty deal conceives another. I won't be a party to it. I have some pride left —."

"Just this once, Stanley. For me. I promise it'll be the last."

"Promises! Why should I believe you'd mean it now. No, Mac, if you do any more of this underhanded stuff, you'll do it on your own. And I'm warning you, I won't protect you!"

"You don't have to. I'll get by, and do as I please too. Nothing can stop me now. Nothing."

As she talked her voice grew softer, deeper, as she lashed out at him in her anger. She knew that he had at last reached bottom. As her temper became more intense so did her language.

Stan had never seen Mac like this before. It was all the hate and fury of hell unleashed.

His eyes were sad as he left and closed the door upon this obscene picture. As he leaned wearily against the closed door, Paul, his young son, peered from his bedroom door, frightened and aghast. He couldn't stop now, it would only have added fuel to the fire. He hurried down the long stairs. Mac had always been jealous of Paul. It would do no good to draw her spite to the boy.

MacAllister came from the room like a tiger stalking its prey. The box of powder she had been holding in her hand exploded in a cloud of white on the wall in back of him. It had a clinging scent, the heavy odor of violets. He walked into his combination library and den and shut the sliding door. Mac had fixed up her bedroom on the first floor so that she could have privacy. Stan's bedroom was on the second floor, next to Paul's. The library was his haven, where he worked far into the early morning hours, after his regular hours at his downtown office.

As he shut the door he leaned wearily against it. Life had suddenly become empty of all meaning and he felt nothing. Not pity nor sorrow for himself, nor for Mac.

He sat at his desk for a long time. Then, slowly, weighing each word before committing it to paper, he wrote. Later, still dazed and tired beyond all belief, he put down his pen.

As he finished he breathed a deep, jagged sigh. I can't believe that I've done it. This finishes things between Mac and me. I didn't think I'd have the courage to face her or that she'd let me off the hook. But Kari and Rock won't get mixed up in this.

He reached in his watch pocket to make sure the tiny nitro-tablets were there. His exploring finger touched the small container. It was there, and full. He relaxed in his chair.

# CHAPTER SEVEN

"Yes, I sent Rock that snapshot because I wanted to brag a little, I guess." Stanley Norton admitted to his client. He frowned at himself. Why did she make him feel shy? He knew many beautiful women. He was an elgible young widower with one young son. Why did this good-looking redhead make him feel shy? Because he had won his first big case, defending her against the spiteful accusations of the highschool board, forcing them to allow her graduation? Because of her refusal to run away with that neurotic jerk of a teacher, who then swallowed enough carbon monoxide from a garden hose and a running-automobile engine to run away from his wife and three children and life?

"I got a letter from Rock — He's still in Germany. He wanted me to tease you." MacAllister laughed.

"Well, you can tell him that you did." said Stan. He handed Mac the tax papers and pointed out the place for

44

her signature, conscious of her nearness and the faint musk of her perfume. Her tax matters were a problem for her that brought them in almost weekly contact. Her war business was booming — all the wives of railroad and boatmen, all the women of all the new offices that dealt with the war effort, seemed to want their hair done at 'MacAllister's'. She had five operators and a male hair stylist.

"There, Stan, that's signed, and you seal and deliver it — but let's dance!" Mac was gay. She stood up and Stan bit his lip as he watched the deep-sprung breasts revealed to him.

He brought her close to him, the flame of her hair just under his chin. The three-piece band of 4F's were in the middle of a rumba, and Stanley Norton, 4F, widower-with-a-son, expertly swung the beautiful girl into the rhythm. His heart was pounding, but not from its normal distress — but a new one. He wanted her as he never had wanted before.

"Does Paul like me Stan?" Mac said, her lips carressed his chin as she spoke. His arm brought her closer for a moment, then away at arms length as she circled him to the sensuous beat of the drums, her hips undulated provocatively as Stan watched in delight.

"Well, Paul doesn't like you as much as I do," he whispered in her hair. Paul was a polite little fellow and if his father liked her than he would too. He would have the most beautiful stepmother in Escanaba. He brought Mac-Allister back to the table, their dinner was waiting.

45

# CHAPTER EIGHT

Bengy Florietto paused before he pushed the doorbell. The sound of mellow chimes came muffled through the heavy paneled door. He pushed the button impatiently. He knew they were home. He pulled the long key chain from his pocket, selected a key and opened the door.

The heavy odor of violets made him wince slightly. What had Mac been trying to do, disinfect the place? With perfume? Then he saw the faint white splotch at the bottom of the stairs where, powder of some kind had been spilled and then vacuumed. He saw the disappearing figure of Signe, the maid, going into the kitchen pushing the cleaner. He shuddered. Mac evidently had thrown another of her famous tantrums. He wondered who had been on the receiving end of this one.

The sound of ice in a cocktail shaker came from the living room. Mac, her sensuous body in its sheath of gold, was mixing.

46

"Bengy?"

"Yes. Ready?"

"Of course."

"Where's Paul? I brought him some funny books."

"I sent him to bed. He was snooping around. Last I saw of him he was sulking.

"Why?"

"Nothing."

"Not another one of your tantrums?"

"And what if it was? He had no business sticking his head out. Anyway," she closed her eyes until they were mere slits, "I won't have him looking at me like that."

"Mac, Mac, will you ever learn? Paul's a sensitive boy. Those tantrums are enough to scare the living daylights out of anyone! Why can't you understand and treat him accordingly?" He looked around the room then. "Is Stan about ready?"

"He's not going."

"Not going?"

"No, he's not feeling well." She filled the glasses and put them in Bengy's hands. "Stan likes a shot. I'll bring it in. He's in the library."

"I thought Doc said no alcohol for a while?" Mac frowned at him as she answered, "One won't hurt him."

The door stood open and they walked in, Bengy with the cocktails and MacAllister with a shot-glass of brandy and a wash. Stan was sitting quietly at his huge, paper-strewn desk, his eyes closed. He didn't open them.

"It's no use, Mac," he began but Mac interrupted before he could finish.

"I've brought you a drink, Stan. Bengy's here."

Stan opened his eyes then and smiled grimly at the hairdresser.

47

"Hello, Bengy. Guess you're in on the latest."

"Yes, he's in on it," Mac answered quickly before Bengy could ask what he meant.

But Bengy was curious. "In on what?"

"The finals —"

Bengy looked at MacAllister for some sort of explanation. Not finding any he said vaguely, "Sure, sure." He was a little surprised at the smile on Stan's face.

"Yes, the finals, the finale, Bengy. After a long third act there's always the curtain."

"Let's not be melodramatic, Stan. The least we can do is to be friends. Here, let's drink to it." She paused, then placed the shot-glass in his hand.

"Friends!" Stan tossed off the forbidden drink and spat the words out again. "Friends! And tell me, how can that be managed?" A look of pain shot through his pale, thin face and his hand reached for his collar.

Bengy hurried to his side. "Quick, Mac, get me some water."

"Let him alone, Bengy. He'll snap out of it."

Stan was fumbling at his vest pocket when his wife reached him and he made no move as she dipped her cerise-tipped fingers in and pulled out the small plastic pill box.

His eyes followed her movements as she clenched her fingers tightly around the tiny container. His mouth was open slightly and his breath was short and irregular.

"Quick, Mac, the nitro!" Bengy held out his hand.

MacAllister backed away to the cocktail shaker and, with a deliberate, quick flip of the cover, emptied the contents of the pill box into the liquid.

Bengy gasped, stunned, unable to move. "Mac!"

Almost unintelligable words came from Stan's lax lips, "Never escape her — never — tell Rock —"

He seemed to slide down, to settle comfortably in the huge chair

"For God's sake, Mac, are you insane? Get the doctor!" He grabbed the cocktail shaker and ineffectually tried to pour some of the liquid into the lax mouth. The liquid ran down Stan's chin onto his clothes.

Tearing at Stan's shirt and coat, Bengy felt for a pulse. "He's still breathing! Hurry, Mac!"

But Mac continued to stand and to look.

The sound of a door slamming somewhere in the house broke the silence. It was a muffled, dulled sound, ending with a thud.

Bengy tried to revive Stan, finally moved away from the desk.

"Mac —" the horror in his voice as he looked at her was almost childlike in its intensity. "Do you realize you've killed him, Mac?"

But MacAllister only smiled grimly as she answered, "He died upstairs. He asked for it himself. He said he was through. You know what that would mean, Bengy —"

Bengy picked up the telephone and was about to dial when she snatched it from his hand and replaced it.

"We've got to get the doctor! I can't stand this, we can bring him out of it if we hurry!"

"No, Bengy. For me. You wouldn't do that to me, would you? He'll tell them everything." She half-lidded her eyes and the words were soft. She moved to his side and the odor of violet was like a heady wine.

"But murder, Mac! That was not what I wanted!"

"Can we help it if he didn't have his nitro-pills handy? Of course not. They'll never know, unless you tell them."

She looked around and saw the highball glasses, the cocktail shaker. "I'll get rid of these," she walked to the

49

kitchen. The glasses clinked together in her hands as she hurried out with them. The sound of water running and the sound of cupboard doors closing came to him. Somewhere in the house he could hear a dog barking. Probably Paul's huge mongrel pet, Mr. McTavish.

It seemed only a moment before she was back.

She pushed him away from the desk.

"Let's get out of here. We'll be late at the club as it is."

Bengy, with the odor of violets heavy in his nostrils, knew that he could not stop this woman.

"But Mac —" he had to protest anyway.

"No! No calls. We've got to get out of here. We must not be late for the dinner."

"What if someone comes?"

"Who would come?" Anyway, we'll shut and lock the door, turn out the lights. If anyone comes around they'll think there's no one home."

"And Paul?" Bengy looked nervously from Stan to Mac.

"He's asleep. Must be. He was bawling when I left him. Knows better than to get up!"

"But what if he comes down, and calls the doctor? And what if Stan talks?"

Bengy'd dark eyes were almost popping from his slate grey face.

"Don't worry." Mac purred. "He'll never talk, he'd better not!"

# CHAPTER NINE

Kari hesitated before the door inscribed with elegant gold letters, Stanley Norton, Attorney-at-Law. They were plain, but impressive and a bit awesome. She pushed the door open hesitantly. Perhaps the should have waited at the hotel for Rock. Maybe he was back there wondering where she had gone. But he'd been gone much too long.

The door shut automatically behind her and the secretary looked up from her work.

"Yes? May I help you?"

"Is Doctor Harris here with Mr. Norton?"

The secretary frowned slightly. "Dr. Harris? Why no. He was here earlier but left."

"Is Mr. Norton here?" Kari was beginning to feel a bit absurd. After all the secretary was working after hours. She'd no business interrupting, the woman looked tired, weary.

"He left some time ago." The answer was brief.

"Thank you. Do you know where I might find him?"

" I believe he was going home. May I have your name?"

"Oh, I'm sorry. Kari Brent."

The woman smiled for the first time then. "Oh yes, Rock's fiancee. We grew up together. But," she hesitated a moment, I'd take him and run, far away from Escanaba, if I were you —"

She seemed to realize she'd said more than she should. She dismissed Kari with a nod and turned back to her typewriter.

"Thank you, good night." Kari leaned against the door as she closed it tight behind her. The sound of the typewriter keys clicking came to her from within.

Why had this woman, Stan's secretary, told her to go — to run she'd said. First Stan had said it.

She might as well go back to the hotel and wait. It was no use looking for Rock. Maybe she'd see him on her way back to the hotel.

As she walked back down Ludington Street she was aware of glances from passersby, perhaps she was over self-conscious she thought. Why would they look at her?

The old gentleman coming out of the bank tipped his hat to her and smiled. They all were curious about the young woman he was going to marry. It was a warm feeling, knowing that she was recognized here by the fact she belonged to Rock, was his girl. Her smile became permanent as she passed other curious people and they all seemed to react the same, to smile and speak.

At the hotel desk again, she waited for the clerk to turn to her.

"Miss Brent," and he fished the key from 317 and handed it to her with a flourish.

52

She hurried to the elevator. Maybe he'd left a note.

It was much later when the call came through. Lights on Ludington Street were beginning to break through the gloom.

"Yes? Rock?"

"Darling! Someone saw you on the street and I've been looking for you. I've a date with Stan. Meet me at his home, just follow Ludington Street to Lake Shore Drive and then down a few blocks. I'll meet you there. They're going to the club for dinner so we'll have to hurry."

"But Rock —"

"It's that great big old house with the white pillars, darling — you can't miss it. Be a good girl and hurry."

"All right. I'll be there by the time you are. Bye."

A fresh make-up took but a moment, a touch of lipstick and a flip of the brush. She'd already spent the past hour alternating between pacing and brushing the thick blonde hair to a fluffy perfection. She could see the last faint rays of the sunset and she reached the street again.

Her steps were quick as she walked down to the point where Ludington and Lake Shore Drive merged. It was almost dark now and the cool of evening was held in by the overhanging arbor of maple trees. Crickets chirped here in the close cropped grass of the park along the shore.

Most of the homes along the drive were lighted and Kari watched for the one with white pillars. She saw several but they did not seem to fit Rock's description. She almost passed it before Rock's voice called to her.

"The house is dark. They must have gone on!"

Kari hugged his arm close to her.

"Let's go back to the hotel then —" she looked at the deepening shadows and shivered.

"No, Stan said he'd wait for me. Maybe in the back of the house, the library possibly. There's a light on somewhere, I saw it from the street as I came along."

"Looks pretty dark to me!"

As they approached the house together Kari was aware of all the night sounds and conscious of the house and its spectral columns looming up into an overhead, unroofed porch. A cupola hung precariously at the left hand corner of the second story.

She peered through the gloom, still wondering at her unusual dread. Only the firm, strong arm within her grasp seemed real. She tensed suddenly at a thud. Then a dog barked.

The thud sounded like a door closing, maybe a window. But it sounded close, somewhere overhead.

They climbed the long steps and crossed between the heavy white pillars to the dark oak door and Rock pushed the doorbell. They could hear the deep musical chime — loud enough to be heard throughout the entire house. It seemed to echo and re-echo in the thick silence.

After a long moment, pregnant with unspoken fears, Rock said. "He said he'd be here. I don't understand it. It isn't like him to stand anyone up!"

"Perhaps he met someone, maybe there's word at the hotel for you —"

Rock shook his head and she could see the pale blur of his white face as it moved from side to side.

"No. He said he'd be here. You can depend on him. Come — let's go around to the library."

He picked their way carefully across the darkened porch

again and around the corner of the house holding Kari's hand in his. They saw a pale light coming from a window toward the rear of the house, in an L-shaped wing. It was open a few inches. Standing beneath it, his head just reaching the top of the low sill, Rock called out, "Stan! Stan!" but ther was no answer. They could hear the dull clack of a pendulum clock from within the room.

Feeling around experimentally with his foot for a toe hold, Rock found an outdoor faucet. With this to help him he pulled himself up.

"God!" The exclamation seemed torn from the depths, then he dropped to the ground.

"There's a screen on that damn window but I'm sure I saw a body on the floor!"

"A body" Kari's voice was alarmed.

"It will take me longer to get that screen off than to go through the basement. Come on!"

Somehow Kari followed Rock in the blackness. It was more by instinct than sight and her fear kept mounting with every step.

A muffled curse came to her from the dark. "I found it. Almost broke my neck!" The sound of creaking hinges added another chill producing noise and the smell of mildew and dampness rushed out at them.

Rock fumbled for his lighter. The bright flame flickered on five steps leading down into the basement. Kari stumbled along behind him.

"I've played cops and robbers here hundreds of times," Rock said, "come, here are the steps to the first floor." He held his hand out to her.

A moment later they were in the dimly-lit library. Her eyes were following the beam of the torch as Rock smung it back and forth across the room. When it reached the desk, it moved past then came back to the form on the floor. He was beside the prostrate man then, kneeling beside him feeling for a pulse.

"Stan — Oh my God! He's not dead!" Kari's voice broke with tension.

"No. His heart's beating —" Rock fumbled around in the pockets of Stan's coat. "Where the devil are his nitro-pills?"

His search was fast but thorough, and it revealed nothing. Then he was dialing the police. He handed the telephone to Kari. "Explain to them just what we found. I'm going to look around. Those pills must be someplace. Then call the doctor." He was was gone before Kari could protest or ask questions and she explained as best she could, about Stan to the police and requested an ambulance in almost the same breath.

She could hear Rock in the kitchen as she hung up the phone. She heard the water running, splashing noisily in the sink, she heard the slam of a kettle as it banged against the faucet and the gurgling of the water as it gushed into the emptiness. The slam of a cupboard door came to her as she called out — "What doctor shall I call, Rock?" and heard him answer, "Dr. Hallfrisch. You'll find his number there in the front of the book. Stan always kept it handy."

It was there and she could hear the steady ringing at the other end of the line. There was a click, then, "Dr. Hallfrisch speaking."

Rock came back from the gitchen then and she handed the phone to him. His face seemed strong and tense in the dim light of the library.

He reached for a small bottle on the desk, half-hidden by disarranged papers. "I've found something here, it's

56

number 36492 — from Greggs Pharmacy. Would that be it? Yes. It just says place one under tongue whenever necessary. But it's empty, Doc! No, there's nothing else here that I can see. It must be what he always carries with him. Yes, I won't do anything. But hurry, Doc!"

The telephone clicked in it's cradle and Rock put the bottle back on the desk. "He said not to move him. Just leave him alone, quiet.

"How long will it take him to get here?"

"A couple minutes. God — he looks like he suffered through hell and back! He's thinner than he was.

"Better call the police back and tell them to find Mac." Rock's voice was clipped, short.

"Mac?"

"Stan's wife. They'll find her. She's probably out at a dinner somewhere. They'll know where she is."

Kari spoke briefly to the police. "She's at a dinner."

"I knew they would know."

"What's she like?"

"What's who like?" Rock passed a clenched fist across his forehead, the perspiration stood in beads until he brushed them away.

"His wife. Did you call her Mac?"

"MacAlister."

"What's she like?"

"That would be a hard question for me to answer, Kari. You see, darling, she is part and parcel of the past I wanted to talk to you about. You see, when I left to go overseas, we were engaged — at least I thought we were. But Stan came along. He didn't know about me. He had money, position. Everything that I didn't have. I wrote to Stan and played the wronged fiance. I haven't seen him since to straighten things out." His voice broke.

"Stan must have known, Rock. He talked to me in his

57

office. He was anxious to see you, too. He was your true friend, Rock. He knows you love me and he knows how much I love you."

Rock pulled her to him for an instant and held her tight. His lips were against her face as he whispered, desperately, "I've never loved anyone like I love you, darling. Mac was like a flame. She fascinated me and I thought it was love. It's something I can't explain, something I want to forget. I was young, but that's no excuse." He pushed her gently away then and knelt beside Stan.

Kari shuddered and closed her eyes. They were helpless. They must wait for the doctor.

That was when she noticed the cocktail shaker on the desk. It was empty. There were no glasses around. It looked out of place. "Funny thing to have sitting on the desk, with no glasses," she said, to break the stillness.

Rock looked up then. "Yeah, that is strange. You know Stan couldn't touch a drop. Doctor's orders!"

Kari moved to the desk now and picked up the shaker. Only a few drops were visible in the bottom. She held it to her nose. "Funny smell," she observed.

"What do you mean?" Rock was on his feet now holding out his hand for the shaker. He took it from her and held it to his nose. Then tipped it up so that the dorps of liquid would run to the top. He touched his tongue to the rim and let a drop slide to where he could taste it.

"Horrible tasting stuff," he said and replaced the shaker on the desk. He knelt beside Stan again, trying to find a pulse. "I wish the doctor would get here. If anything happens to Stan—" his voice shook. He was like a brother to me, Kari. He kept me straightened out more than once. He'd never mentioned his childhood to Kari.

"He told me he liked you, Rock. That you can be sure of."

"And I liked him. His word was law as far as I was concerned." He hesitated to swallow the lump that threatened to cut off his voice. "More law than my father ever was. All I remember about him is that he was—an alcoholic —a pathetic alcoholic. Boozed it up every chance he had . . . until he died in the charity ward with the D.T.'s.

Kari couldn't stand the deep hurt he was revealing to her. She slid her arm around his shoulder and pressed her face into the top of his hair.

"Don't, darling, don't crucify yourself like this. The past is gone, bringing it back won't help anything.

"But when I think of the things I wrote to him—of the things I said, I could cut my tongue out. And all over Mac. He loved her I know. And she used him to get her way. She didn't love him. Poor Stan, he didn't deserve a rotten break like that."

"Don't Rock, —" Kari put her finger to his lips.

Rock pulled it away and held her hand gently in his as he looked at her. "If only he hadn't loved her so much—the hurt wouldn't go so deep. He must have gone through hell. And if I know Mac—she sure put him through it, over and over."

The moment stretched into minutes as they stayed there beside Stan. Silent now, Rock held Kari's hand in his, other hand anxiously holding Stan's wrist, counting each faint beat of pulse.

Then it came. The sound of the ambulance siren. They could hear it as it turned from the main street and came swiftly down the drive. Kari was at the door to open it as they ran up on the porch. The doctor, young and serious, pushed past her with the question, where is he?"

She pointed to the library. He obviously knew his way in this house because he asked nothing more of her. Two men in hospital white followed him down the hall, then a man in uniform ran up the steps. She hurried along after him until they reached the door to the library.

At the door he stopped and blocked Kari's way. "You can't go in there now, Miss," his voice was firm.

"But I've been in there all the time," she objected.

But he shook his head, entered the library and closed the door after him. Kari could hear the rise and fall of voices, Rock's and the others, intermingled. She couldn't tell what they were saying, but Rock seemed to be disturbed and she could tell from the tone of his voice that he was angry.

She could hear them moving furniture across the polished floor. She paced back and forth in front of the closed door and tried to picture what they were doing. One of the men in white went out to the ambulance but returned immediately with something she couldn't distinguish in his hand.

It was while she paced the hallway, back and forth, finally to the front near the long stairway and back that she noticed the white spot on the carpeting. It looked like something had been spilled and hastily vacuumed. She bent over the spot and rubbed her hand across it. It seemed to stir a faint scent. Powder she thought, conscious of the lingering odor on her hand. Funny thing to be spilled in the hallway, especially right near the front door.

She stopped near the door, trying to place the scent, when the man in uniform came out of the library. She hurried back to speak to him.

He blocked the doorway as he closed the door behind him.

"How is he?"

In the long pause that followed, Kari felt a chill, a premonition of something evil. The man was looking at her now, searching her face for something. "He's pretty bad. The doctor can't tell. He's breathing and that's about all. I am Wesley Bjornquist. Police. Now, I want you to tell me what happened."

"I don't know much except that Rock and I found him—"

"You didn't come with Rock?"

"No."

"You met him here?"

"Yes."

"Had he been here long? Did he come from the house?"

"No, of course not. He couldn't get in. The door was locked."

"Is that what he told you?"

"Of course that's what he told me. I know he was here only seconds before I got here."

"How do you know?"

"I just know he wasn't, that's all."

"But it was dark, wasn't it?"

"Yes. It was dark . . ."

"Well, then if he'd have come from behind the house you wouldn't have seen him . . . ?"

"No. I suppose not."

"Then he could have come from the back of the house?"

"Well—" Kari hated to agree, "I suppose he could have."

Wesley Bjornquist held up his hand to stall the next words. He put his finger to his lips. It sounded like someone crying, whimpering.

"It sounds like a baby crying. But there's no one here—"

"It sounds like it's coming from upstairs someplace." Bjornquist pushed past her and hurried to the stairway. She saw that he hadn't noticed the spot of white on the carpet as she followed close on his heels. She almost stumbled when he stopped suddenly on the top step and listened.

The crying, sobbing, came clearer. It was very close, behind one of the doors. Kari shuddered in the darkness and tried to find the light switch with her hand. Suddenly she found it and pressed the button. A huge domed light in the center of the long, wide hallway cast its soft brilliance down upon them. Several family portraits hung in gilt frames over marble-top lowboy chests of drawers.

Wesley motioned for her to stay away while he moved off quietly down the hall toward the sound. He tried two doors. They swung inward revealing nothing but the darkness. The third door was locked. He turned the lock gently and the crying stopped abruptly. Then the beating of fists on the door startled them.

Bjornquist pushed Kari back, she had come up close to him, and then turned the door knob. The door swung inward, this time on a lighted room. There, fists upraised, ready to attack the door again, stood a boy, obviously frightened. His eyes had a look of terror in them as he stared at the two strange people. Small of stature, with a light curly crew-cut, the child must have been about nine years old. His face was tear-streaked and red, and he was still sobbing, a frightened, body-wracking sound.

"The door was locked," he whimpered, "somebody locked me in," then the tears began to flow again and he darted past them, evidently afraid they might lock him in his room again. He seemed to hardly touch the stairs as he made his dash for the library, screaming, "Daddy, Daddy—"

One of the men in white stood just outside the door and grabbed him before he could enter. The youngster fought and kicked but could not break free. The man kept talking to him, trying to calm him down.

Kari wondered then just why the child had been locked in his room. This was Stan's young son she was sure. But who had locked the door from the outside? In the house alone, with the door locked frm the outside. Kari was sure that Stan wouldn't have done it. But if not Stan, then who?

She walked down the long stairway asking herself these questions. Rock was just coming out of the library, looking around for her. Kari ran down the last few steps and was about to call to him, when the front door swung in and a woman stood within the frame. The glitter of the light on her gold lame gown made her stand out as a flame-topped candle. Her hair, fiery red, fell in beautiful, soft waves around her face. Here was beauty, Kari thought, raw, savage beauty. A predatory animal, not too far removed from its natural state, sensuous, small, commanding attention and getting it from everyone in the hallway. Not a word was spoken.

She nodded briefly to Wesley then, and closed the door behind her. Now she walked toward Rock until she stood in front of him, only a breath away, and looked up into his eyes. She smiled at him then and he closed his eyes for a moment to break the spell. His face was deathly white.

Kari started toward Rock. Then MacAllister saw her and was about to speak when the tall, dark haired man came in from the porch. He stumbled a little and it was obvious that he had been drinking. Kari turned back to MacAllister.

"We've just let your child out of his room. He was locked in."

"Paul. But what was he locked in for . . . and all alone here? You must be mistaken."

"No, we are not mistaken, Mrs. Norton. Paul was locked in his room."

MacAllister looked at Wesley Bjornquist then, eyebrows raised in question. He nodded.

The dark man was in front of her now, staring into her face, his eyes held a strange look in them. Kari wasn't sure whether it was pity, horror or anger. Perhaps not any of these things, but something, she wasn't sure what. She said, "I'm Kari Brent, Rock's fiancee."

"Oh—oh yes, Miss Brent. I'm Benjamin Florietto, I manage Mac's—er—Mrs. Norton's Beauty Salon."

Rock saw her then. He'd been talking with MacAllister, his lips tense and white. Kari had never seen him look like this. He seemed angry, disturbed too, but angry.

He motioned to her to come closer. "Kari, this is MacAllister." He nodded at Bengy. "Bengy—"

MacAllister turned slightly, toward Kari. She made no attempt to speak at first. Kari could feel the contempt for her in Mac's blue eyes as she briefly looked her over.

"Of coure I'll need your fiance —" the sarcasm in her voice was definitely barbed, "Rock and I have been close —" she squeezed Rock's arm, "close friends for a long, long time.

Rock seemed to shrink away from the words and he looked at Kari as if to say "Please understand . . ."

Kari closed her eyes for a moment. This voice. This velvet voice — she had heard it before. The voice who'd called Rock at the hotel.

# CHAPTER TEN

The group around Stan Norton's bed waited and watched silently. MacAllister — stood at the end of the bed alone. Her eyes were partly closed as if she were concentrating, her red hair gleamed like the mythical Medusa.

Kari stood in the hall near the door into the room. Only the close relatives were allowed in the sick room. Rock, because he was his best friend, MacAllister and Paul, and Wesley Bjornquist.

Poor Paul, Kari watched him through the small opening of the almost closed door. He seemed so small and frail and so frightened. Doctors hurried in and out of the room with hypos and worried looks. They said very little and the strain on the little group was beginning to be visible in the tight-drawn expressions on their faces.

MacAllister stood rigid, there in the sterile white of

the room and Kari could feel the hate pour from the small body. She looked again to make sure it wasn't her imagination.

She is willing him to die, Kari thought, you can see it in every move she makes, every glance she gives him from behind those half-closed eyelids.

Kari looked at the policeman. He was much more interested in watching for signs of consciousness in the patient than he was in watching the faces of the small gathering. But Kari could watch, she could almost read the thoughts aloud. Bengy stood across the hall from her. He looked like a man with something on his mind. Kari wondered if he were hoping Stan would die too.

Then her eyes went back to MacAllister. The changing expressions of degrees of hate were almost unbelieveable in their intensity. Her lips moved and Kari was almost sure she was saying, "Die, die," and she watched her mouth this one word over and over again until she could almost hear it.

Everyone else was intent on the face of the struggling man, trying to come back from the outer fringe of life. There was a brief movement as Stan gasped for breath and Kari knew he was far away from them. She could feel it, they all could feel it. The doctor motioned for a hypodermic from the attendant who stood at his side.

"If he can come out of this," the doctor looked at MacAllister and then stared at her as she stood there oblivious to his words, "he might have a chance," he finished and turned his eyes away from her.

Kari could see MacAllister's hands tighten their grip on the metal foot of the bed. Kari moved from the doorway and was aware that the attendant had motioned Paul out of the sick room. He motioned for her to watch him. The room was no place for this small boy.

"Come, Paul," Kari put her arm around his shoulder and walked with him to a chair in the hall. The child was shaking with tears and grief and she did her best to quiet him. Even though she closed her eyes she could still see Mac's lips repeating, "Die! Die!"

Several minutes later Rock came out of the room. His face was white. He answered her unspoken question.

"They just can't tell yet. It doesn't look good. It's as though there's an evil force at work against which he has no protection.

Kari knew what the evil force was. Mac. But Kari couldn't tell Rock this.

Then Rock looked into her eyes and for a moment they were alone. His look caressed her and she no longer was afraid.

He stroked Paul's head for an instant as if to give the boy strength. Then he was gone again. Back to the room across the hall.

"Everything will be all right, Paul." Kari tried to give what comfort she could but the boy sat silently, stiffly at her side, his face half turned toward the door of the room across the hall. His eyes were red from weeping.

"No. It won't be all right."

"They are doing everything for him. He'll get well."

"No." The words came out, clipped, emotionless, "He'll die, I know."

Kari shivered as these cold words came from this slight, frightened boy. Bengy, across the hall, heard the words too and Kari was sure his face blanched as he watched the small boy. Then his eyes turned back to the door and the drama being enacted within. The attendant had left the door wide open now and Kari could see MacAllister from where she sat.

Kari watched her now. She seemed to be as nervous as Bengy. They both were fidgeting, Bengy in the hallway outside and MacAllister at the foot of the bed. Kari could hear the labored breath from where she sat. MacAllister acted as if she wished it were all over. She didn't look at him now.

Then Kari saw Rock move closer to the bed and MacAllister walked close to him and began whispering. Rock's face remained immobile and he didn't look at Mac.

Two of the doctors came out of the room and crossed to where she sat with Paul. Bengy moved closer to hear what they were going to say.

"Stan will be all right?" Kari asked.

"It's a little early to tell. He didn't have his pills handy."

"His pills?"

"Nitro. Every heart patient carries a small vial of nitro-tablets in his pocket. That's what I don't understand."

When he said this Kari saw Bengy stiffen. Is he hoping that Stan will die? Is that it? "But is he better?" she continued.

"I wouldn't say better." The doctor hesitated, "but he may snap out of it. That's what we're hoping for. If we can only keep his heart working he has a chance. If only they'd called sooner —"

Again Kari was aware that Bengy was jittery. She looked at him and he started almost as if someone had pointed an accusing finger at him . . .

He stood up and moved toward the door of the room across the hall.

The doctor stepped in front of him. "No one except the family," he explained.

Kari saw Bengy stiffen, then put out his hand to push

the doctor aside. "I've got to see Mac — she needs me —"

"No." The doctor stood his ground.

"I must." Bengy leaned forward on the balls of his feel as though he might slug it out with the doctor.

But the doctor turned and walked away ignoring him. This did more than words could have and Bengy returned to his chair against the corridor wall and slumped into it.

Kari felt sorry for Bengy somehow. One had only to look at him to knew that he loved MacAllister. She was standing close to Rock, whispering, trying to command his attention but he had eyes only for Stan.

Kari was deep in thought when Paul went limp in her arms. The tense, tightness against her shoulder relaxed and a shuddering sigh escaped the pale lips of the child at her side. Paul slept, at peace at last, She could not understand how Mac could be so unthinking, so resentful of the care of Paul. Actually, from all Kari could gather, Mac did resent Paul. It was as if she actually hated the child.

What had put that expression of terror — of fear on the face of this child, Kari wondered. There was a haunting look of uncontrollable hate intermingled with fear when the child looked at either Mac or Bengy. He would have said something if there had been any reason behind it. Kari sat quietly, her arm around the slight body, glad to be able to give comfort, glad to be needed.

Movement within the room across the hall attracted Kari's attention. She could see Rock talking with the intern. The doctor was not visible from where Kari sat. But she could see Mac. She was no longer staring at the figure in the hospital bed.

Wesley Bjornquist, sitting near the head of the bed,

was relaxed, napping, waiting. Kari watched the tableau before her. Mac, looking first at Wesley then at Rock and seeing that no one was paying any attention to her, stood up. Her movements were feline, and Kari could see her eyes darting first at one then the others in the room.

She moved to the head of the bed and bent over Stan. It happened quickly. Mac stood up again and as she did she looked out into the hallway. Kari was staring at her.

Mac shrugged and returned to her place at the foot of the bed. The doctor, who had been out of Kari's vision until now, bent over his patient. Kari could see him feel for Stan's pulse then call the intern. A hypodermic was put into his hand. It was no use. The doctor shook his head slowly. There were no words spoken. Rock leaned his head back against the wall for a moment. His best friend was dead.

Bengy, sitting across the hall from Kari, had been watching.

As the doctor turned away, Bengy, who had been sitting on the edge of his chair, collapsed. He leaned over, head in hands, and Kari could see the deep shudder go through his body. She had not realized the extent of his tension until then. Her shoulders were numb from Paul's weight on her shoulder and she moved him gently and rose to meet Rock who was coming to her now.

At the door of the room he hesitated. MacAllister had stepped in front of him now and was talking to him. He paid no attention to her. He was looking into Kari's eyes and she could see the deep hurt, the anguish he was feeling. Mac turned then when she realized he wasn't even hearing what she was saying. The expression on her face, as well as Bengy's, was one of relief. She hadn't even met her until today. Kari knew that this was all mixed up

70

with Bengy, with Mac, and with Rock. That she, as an outsider, could see what Rock couldn't see.

Rock was before her now. His face a mask. He'd heard nothing that Mac had said to him. Just before she went into his arms, Kari looked at Mac. She knew now the meaning of the phrase "the law of the jungle" with all it implied.

Suddenly she was frightened. More frightened than she'd ever been in her life. She knew there was danger here. Danger for her. Danger for Rock, because of her. She looked at Bengy. He hadn't moved. But his eyes were on MacAllister.

# CHAPTER ELEVEN

The nip of fall was in the air this morning. Bustle and activity on the waterfront indicated that the rush season for ore handling was close at hand and diesels were working round the clock to push ore into the open, yawning caverns that were the holds of the lake freighters. The sun, bright in a cloudless sky, created latticelike shadows on the water below as it cut through the open crossbeams of the docks.

It cut horizontal shadows into the crowded coroner's inquest room at the court house, giving those who sat in its glow the effect of being clothed in prison stripes.

The crowd was getting restless. MacAllister, arriving with a great deal of staging, sat at the front of the room. Her gown for the occasion was charcoal black, fitted to her feline shape with pre-designed care, subdued, yet suggestive. Even in the black of mourning, she had difficulty in keeping the volcano from showing through.

She brushed aside the veil covering her face, and covered her eyes for a momet with the lacy whisp of handkerchief. She must not let them suspect that there was anything more than routine to this investigation. She would have to act at being the mourning widow for the benefit of the press, radio and TV reporters. It would never do for them to catch her off guard after she had planned this whole thing so carefully. She must give them the impression that all she wanted was the truth, and — of course — justice. She must not let them see the tension which was inside her.

Of course everything would be all right. There was no reason for it to turn out otherwise. She had everything under control, no one except Bengy knew what had happened and Bengy wouldn't talk. She turned to look at him. He looked terrible this morning. Dark circles under his eyes gave proof that he'd not slept well. MacAllister wished he didn't have to go on the stand.

Actually, everything had gone along very well, so far. The autopsy, the doctor's report, witnesses. Everything had clicked. Just as she'd planned it would.

Wesley Bjournquist was on the stand now. His words droned on and on. He was making the most of it. Election-grass-roots. MacAllister brushed her eyes again with her handkerchief. She must remember to be the grieving widow of Stanley Morton.

MacAllister watched Wesley. He was dragging out his testimony . . . and people were beginning to whisper and move about, restlessly. She turned to face the audience so that she could see what they were doing. They were looking at her instead of the man on the stand. Her eyes

73

flicked from face to face. She could read a variety of emotions. Admiring glances on many of the men's faces, some familiar and some strange. It gave her a great deal of satisfaction to see the way she affected men. Most of the women had either sympathy or envy displayed in their glances. A few, the ones she knew very well, had hate for her written openly on their faces. The corner of her mouth twitched as she controlled the urge to smile. .

This was all going according to plan. A long range plan that began back in her school days. The days when she lived on the North shore road. Squalor, filth, and decadence had been all around her in her school years. She had been made aware of it when the school children had mocked and jeered, when they had pointed at her and sing-songed "North shore white trash, north shore white trash —" She still had nightmares in which she ran wildly along the white, sandy beach of Lake Michigan and screamed to get rid of the hated words . . . North shore white trash, north shore white trash . . . north shore white trash.

When she left school, she had only one focal point ahead. To return to Escanaba and make them eat their words.

Beauty School, hair-styling school, extra courses, all in the fine art of making women beautiful, then her return. She had developed all of her charms, all of her potentials until she was the alluring, the illusive MacAllister Heminger. She had set her cap for Rock. He had been captivated by her sleek beauty, her sensual appeal, her magnetic personality. The war had upset her plans. She could not wait for Rock. Her program did not include waiting for any soldier who might or might not come back. So she had set her sights on Stan Norton, prominent young lawyer and Rock's friend. He had not known how serious Rock

74

was about MacAllister. Not until long after they were married. Not until he'd received the letter from Rock. Then it was too late. Too late for many things.

Her position in Escanaba had risen to new heights then. She not only had the most fashionable shop in the city but she had one of the best homes and entry into the elite crowd. She made them all eat crow. It had given her a great deal of satisfaction. She, MacAllister Heminger, from the north shore, figuratively the other side of the tracks, had made good. Damn good! She purred inside, like the feline she was. She had the women of Escanaba in the palm of her hand. Choice bits dropped in the shop had made good handles. And she made the most of it. Her prices skyrocketed and the women were afraid not to patronize her. So they paid her prices and patronized her shop. Until the most recent bit of blackmail — until Stan had found out. He'd rebeled. She'd suspected he'd be difficult. But she had thought he'd go along with her. He'd had more spunk than she'd given him credit for. Too bad too. She certainly could have used him. He was an excellent lawyer.

Paul, sitting next to her, pulled away from her side. He'd been sitting quietly until now. Suddenly MacAllister was aware that Paul was being called to the stand. She turned toward him, but he'd eluded her. He didn't even look at her. The officer was leading him to the chair near the coroner. He sat down. His face was pale and drawn.

The coroner was leaning across the table now, talking in a low voice to the child. Paul nodded several times then looked at her. For an instant his eyes met hers and she felt a chill settle at the back of her neck. Why?

"Paul?" The coroner was speaking loud enough now for all to hear.

75

The small boy nodded.

"Where were you when your father was taken ill?"

"In my room." The chid's voice was soft but clear.

"And did you hear him call — or hear anything at all?"

Paul stiffened. MacAllister felt the chill move now.

The coroner repeated the question.

Paul closed his eyes. But in a brief flash before they closed he looked at MacAllister. MacAllister knew that she should have talked with Paul before the inquest.

The coroner was waiting for an answer. He spoke again, quietly.

"Well, Paul, did you hear anything?"

Then the child began to talk.

"I heard Mother and Bengy go out. I heard Rock come. I heard him and he called Kari. It was dark but I heard them. I was looking out of the window. My light was out. They didn't see me. Then all the cars came."

"Were you at the window all the time?"

"Yes. I was watching the boats for a while after —" he hesitated and looked at Mac — "after she sent me to my room."

The coroner almost pounced. "Why did she send you to your room?"

Paul seemed to shrink down in the chair. He started to answer then looked at MacAllister.

The damned kid, thought MacAllister. That damned little kid can spoil it all.

"Why did she send you to your room, Paul?" The question came again.

"I had school work to do."

MacAllister leaned back in her chair. Would they be satisfied with his answer? But it was as good an answer as any.

76

She rose slowly, gracefully from her chair. Every eye in the room followed her movements with varied reactions. The photographers were busy now and she took her time walking to the witness chair. She touched her eyes with her handkerchief. Grandstanding, Stan had called this sort of thing. He'd accused her of it so many times in the past few months that she smiled inwardly to herself and played it to the hilt. The people were eating it up. They were tense and sympathetic — all at the same time. They really felt sorry for her. How Stan would have hated her now. She wished he could have seen this. What fools they are, she thought. She paused before she sat down. Let them get one more good picture for the Star Edition.

She was enjoying this. One last touch of the handkerchief to her eyes for effect and a deep sigh. She must look as if she really cared, really mourned Stan.

She answered all the questions. Yes, she was the widow of Stanley Norton. No, she had no idea how it happened. Yes, he was using nitro-pills. No, she had no idea why he hadn't used them. He always carried them with him. Yes, she was sure he had just purchased a new supply. No, she had no knowledge of where they were, where he'd kept them, other than in his pocket. Yes, he was going to the dinner. He planned to meet her there. He'd asked she and Bengy to go on ahead. He'd been perfectly all right when they left him in his study.

"Was there any reason to suspect that he was ill?"

"No, of course not. Otherwise we would not have gone to the dinner."

"Did he say anything to make you think he was not feeling well?"

"No. He was working at his desk when we left."

The coroner paused before he asked the next question.

He held out his hand for one of the exhibits. One of his assistants passed it to him. It was the small prescription bottle.

"Have you ever seen this, Mrs. Norton?"

"Of course. That is the bottle of nitro-pills."

The coroner shook it slightly. "There is nothing in it."

"I suppose it needed refilling. He always carried them in a small pill box in his pocket."

"That, too, was empty."

"I can't understand him being careless about that."

"He was not careless, Mrs. Norton. We checked with the Drug Store. He'd recently had the prescription filled."

"Perhaps he'd used them up. I have no way of knowing how many times he needed them. Stan had attacks and I wouldn't know about them unless someone told me."

"Then how do you explain what happened?"

"I have no idea. Stanley always carried the nitro. He must have been out of them and didn't realize it."

There was a great deal of audience reaction to all this. She could feel the waves of sympathy spread across the room. She could feel that they were in accord with her. She had played her part well. She had made them believe her. She lowered her eyes. Flash bulbs were still going off. Pictures sometimes revealed the truth one could not see with the eye. They were cold, they presented truths.

After a few more such questions, MacAllister returned to her chair in the audience. She was sure everything would be all right after her testimony. She had been careful to watch audience reaction. She could sense that they were all in sympathy with her. It could only have a favorable verdict. Accidental death.

Rock was next on the stand. The coroner continued his

78

questioning in the same vein as he had with all the rest. How did he find the body of his friend? What time did he arrive at the house? Was he alone? When had Kari arrived? What did they do then? It was all there. And more. What did he do when Kari arrived?

"We thought something must be wrong. Stan had made the oppointment to see us. He wouldn't tell us to come and then not be there. That's why we were both suspicious."

"Suspicious?"

"Of course. Stan was not in the habit of making an appointment and then breaking it."

"What did you do when you found the door locked?"

"We walked around the house to see if we could get in."

"How long did that take?"

"Not very long."

"Were any of the doors unlocked?"

"No."

"Then what did you do?"

Rock moved restlessly. "We looked into the room. Tried to see whether he was in there or not. The lights were on and I saw him lying on his desk."

"We went through the cellar door. It is never used but I remembered that we used to play hide and seek there. Luckily we found it unlatched."

"Were you in the house earlier?"

"I was not!"

"Did you or did you not quarrel with your friend?" The coroner knew these answers.

"Yes. But it was of no consequence and had nothing to do with what happened."

"But you had quarreled?"

"Yes. Rather I had quarreled with him." Rock was truthful.

79

The coroner knew that too. Why was he deliberately leading Rock into these questions, MacAllister wondered. In a minute he'll be asking Rock what the quarrel was over. And Rock would be foolish enough to tell him.

"What about the medicine? The nitro pills? Did you see the bottle or the pill box at all?"

"No. They were nowhere to be found. I knew he carried them but they weren't in his pocket."

"Had you ever had the opportunity to see him use them before?"

"No. I haven't seen Stanley for seven years." Rock's voice was flat, without emotion.

"Well then, how did you know he carried nitro pills with him?"

Rock turned to look into the coroner's face. "Even though I had not seen him for a long time I have not been out of contact with the entire family. I have many friends here in Escanaba. Good friends. They've kept me very much aware and informed. I knew when he had his first attack. I also know that Stan, being the methodical and sincere person he was, would have nitro-pills with him. He would never allow a prescription to run out."

He had said all he could say. The coroner dismissed him and sat shuffling papers on his desk while Rock walked back to his seat. The audience whispered behind their hands and moved to more comfortable positions in their chairs.

MacAllister could feel the tension in the room. With the last remark Rock made she had felt the tension building. He wasn't that sort of careless person. How well she knew that. He had always been careful.

She watched Rock walk back to his place. He reminded her of Stan. He and Stan were a great deal alike in many

80

ways. She was aware now that they almost thought alike. They were both careful men. They were not men who would step out of line, or if they did, it would not be for long. They were men with a conscience. *I hate men with a conscience, she thought. Afraid to do what they really want to do for fear they might hurt someone. Too damned good. People don't actually care how much they hurt the other fellow as long as the other fellow didn't find out they knew. If they could make it look unintentional, they were excused.*

It was Bengy's turn on the stand now.

She looked at him. He was hardly aware that his name had been called. *Christ, he looks terrible. I really hadn't noticed until now. I'm so used to looking at him that I didn't realize he'd taken this thing so hard. He actually looks guilty.* She felt herself showing her tenseness. She must sit back, relax. She wished she could help him. Help him relax. But in the last few days since the incident in the library, she could sense the change in him. He'd been hitting the bottle. He'd never been a drinking man. It was as though he were trying to blot out the memory of those few minutes in the library. *Any fool would know that you can't do that with whiskey. It only makes it worse. You have to face facts. You can't run away from them. You can't hide in a bottle.*

Bengy hardly seemed to hear when the coroner began his questioning. He sat looking into space, out over the heads of the audience. The coroner repeated his first question. Bengy came back in thought. His answers were quiet, almost inaudible. The coroner had to ask him, sharply, to speak up.

"Where were you when Mr. Norton was found?"

"I was at the dinner at the club."

"How long had you been there?"

"Not more than half an hour."

"What did you do?"

"I returned to the house with Mrs. Norton."

"Did you see Mr. Norton before you left the house?"

"Yes. He was in the library. He was to join us there in a little while."

"Did he seem to be all right when you left?"

"Yes. Tired perhaps."

MacAllister had rehearsed him well. He was making all the required answers she had coached him on. Robot like, he was doing just as she'd planned for him to do. Some of the tenseness left her now.

"Did he say he had an appointment?"

"No. He didn't mention anything at all. He was busy writing."

"What was he writing?"

"I have no idea." Bengy looked up then. Looked at MacAllister. His eyes had a strange, almost sad look in them —

"Did Stanley always have his nitro-pills with him?"

The hesitation was almost imperceptable. Almost. Mac-Allister caught it immediately and held her breath. *Say you don't know*, she forced this thought on him, *say you don't know!*

"I don't know." The hesitation was gone now. It was replaced by a cold voice, as if MacAllister spoke from his lips.

After a few more questions Bengy was excused. He walked away from the stand with no expression on his face.

*Thank God that's over*, MacAllister pushed back in her chair again, aware that she had been straining forward to hear what Bengy had to say. *I musn't let them see I am nervous. It's almost over now. Only Rock's girl left.* There wasn't anything she could say or do to hurt. It would be death by cause or causes unknown, accidental death. She would be free to carry out the rest of her long range plan.

She'd have these women right where she wanted them — in her little black book. She would have what she wanted. Power — and money. Their money. They'd never turn up their noses at her again. She had planned too long and too well.

Kari was approaching the stand now. She had to admit — that Kari was a lovely girl. Her blonde hair hung in heavy clusters against her neck and curled softly around her face. Yes, Mac could see why Rock would go for this innocent young woman. Her figure was luscious, and she seemed to be completely unaware of it.

The audience watched too. They liked what they saw. They poked each other in the ribs and smiled their approval as Kari walked forward, gracefully, and was seated.

At the first question she smiled and sat back. Her answers were clear and audible. "I'm Kari Brent."

The questions were repetition of all the other and Kari answered them quietly. MacAllister sat waiting for it all to be over. Nothing could hurt her now.

"Yes. I saw Mr. Norton earlier that day. He came to see Rock at the hotel. We had a long visit. He seemed to have a great deal on his mind."

"A great deal?" The coroner as well as the audience leaned forward in their chairs now. MacAllister held her breath. Had Stan told this girl anything?

And then it came out.

"He said that if Rock and I were ever to get married that I should get him out of Escanaba right away. He seemed to be worried about something that would happen if we didn't leave. He mentioned the trial and that he was going to change things. He said that he'd see that we got out." Kari paused. "I didn't know what he meant by it, but that's what he said."

"What did he mean when he said he was going to change things?"

"He was talking about some trial. I guess he was going to leave the case. That's what it seemed like to me."

"Did he actually say he was going to leave the case?"

"Yes. I didn't ask him what he meant. He said Rock would understand."

"And did you tell Rock?"

"I didn't have time to. Everything happened so fast I didn't remember it until right now."

"Are you sure he said," and he quoted, "that he was going to leave the case?"

Kari nodded her head.

*The little bitch. The dirty little bitch! Spoiling everything I've set up. They'll never give it accidental death now.* MacAllister pushed back in her chair, pressed her spine against the unyielding spokes, and cursed Kari and Rock and Bengy. Everything she'd worked for was going up in smoke. *They can't say murder. Not after all the planning I've done. They just can't say murder—*

The jury went into their room.

MacAllister held her hands folded tightly in her lap. She didn't dare unclench them, she was afraid they'd give her away. What was the jury doing behind those doors. Why didn't they come out with the verdict and get it over with. She could almost hear them say . . . Murder! Murder!

And when they did come out she was unprepared for the verdict.

Death by accident—from persons or causes unknown.

84

# CHAPTER TWELVE

Rock pushed the papers away from him as he sat at Stanley's desk. He could hear the clatter of the typewriter as the secretary in the outer office tried to get out some of the reports that had to be taken care of. Rock had been named administrator of Stanley's will by Stanley himself. His last act, sitting there in the library the night of his death was to add a codicil to his will.

It had signed over property to Paul and had cut MacAllister off with only one dollar, but it had not been witnessed. The police had found the extra paper tucked in among the papers as they checked the desk the night Stanley was taken to the hospital. His will had always had Rock on it as executor of the will. That part had not been changed. Of course, now the will would have to stand as it was before the codicil.

Rock ran his fingers through his hair. MacAllister had

been insistent that he and Kari stay at the big house until things had been settled. He had been hesitant about accepting but MacAllister had overruled his feeble answer.

He pushed the buzzer for the secretary. In a moment she came in, notebook in hand.

"You rang," she smiled briefly.

"Yes, Miss McCormick, will you please sit down. I'd like to ask you a few questions if you don't mind."

She sat down beside him at the desk and put her stenographers notebook and pencil in her lap. "Yes?"

"Miss McCormick, how long have you worked for Stanley?"

"It would have been four years next month."

"And during that time you took care of a great many of the details of his correspondence, and business?"

"Yes."

"Did you ever see anything suspicious—like a letter containing threats of any kind?" Rock's face was white.

"Mr. Harris, Mr. Norton was a sincere and good man. He never would do anything to hurt anyone. No, I certainly never saw anything like that go out of this office."

"Did you ever see anything come in the office with money in it—something that had nothing to do with any regular business?"

"I only opened office mail. All personal mail was left unopened and put on his desk."

"Good." Rock smiled now, more relaxed. He was certain that whatever had been going on had been going on through MacAllister.

"Did any mail for Mrs. Norton ever come here to the office?" he asked.

At the mention of MacAllister, the girl's nose tilted slightly and her lips compressed into a thin line.

"Please, Miss McCormick. Don't let any personal feelings enter into the answers. Were there any letters dropped here at the office for Mrs. Norton?"

"Yes. Several times. In fact every so often letters would come in addressed to her in care of the office. They were always marked 'Personal' and came special delivery."

"Did she pick them up?"

"No. Mr. Norton always took care of them. He opened one by mistake one day, I remember it was the first one that ever came like that, and it was full of money, big bills." She swallowed nervously now. "I'm sure he didn't know what they were all about, because he read the short letter and left immediately·afterwards. He didn't come in the rest of the day."

"Did he ever say anything about these letters?"

"No. Nothing."

"Do you like Mrs. Norton?"

"I hate her." She said emphatically.

"Did you ever see him have a heart attack?"

"Yes. Quite a few times lately. I tried to get him to go to the doctor but he always said he was okay, that he had nitro in his pocket and would be all right."

"Did you ever see him take the nitro pill?"

"Oh yes. Lots of times. But he would never let me call the doctor."

"Do you think he had time to get a nitro-pill from his pocket when he felt an attack coming on?"

"Yes. I'm sure he did. He was no fool, Mr. Harris. He was a very smart man. I'm sure it was not an accident. And I know he had plenty of pills because I had the prescription filled for him just a few days before he died." She squirmed in the chair.

"Do you think he would misplace his pill-box?"

"No. I'm sure he wouldn't."

"Then do you think he did it on purpose?"

"I don't know. He'd been acting awfully strange lately."

"Strange? What do you mean?"

"Oh, he seemed to think that his friends were no longer his friends. He used to hate to go down the street. One day he said he felt dirty as he walked among his friends."

Rock stopped the questions for a moment. Why should Stanley feel—as she had said—dirty?

"Do you know what he meant?"

"No. I have no idea. I only know that something real bad must have been troubling him." She hesitated, then continued. "People hate Mrs. Norton, you know. And if I were you I sure wouldn't stay there—I'd be afraid for Miss Brent, too."

"That's ridiculous. What could possibly happen to Miss Brent."

"Yes, I know. I also know, and please forgive me for this, but I also know that Mrs. Norton used to be your girl."

Rock seemed a bit startled at this piece of the past coming from the girl. "But that was a long time ago. I'm sure that Mrs. Norton has other plans now—and I certainly am not interested in what she thinks or does.

"Mrs. Norton has a way of getting what she wants, Mr. Harris. She is a very sly, vindictive person. I'd certainly get Miss Brent out of that house if I were you.

What about this case that he was going to handle for MacAllister?"

"You mean the Jeffries case?"

"Yes. That's the one. What about that case?"

"He didn't want to handle it at all but Mrs. Norton insisted.

"Yes. I know." Rock was agreeing because of all the things he remembered.

"What has been done about the cases on his calendar?"

"They have all been tranferred to Billings and Strong Law Firm. They were friends of Mr. Norton's.

"The Jeffries case too?"

"No. That is one they won't take. I think Mrs. Norton is dealing with them out of court. At least she called and said for me to take it off the calendar and forget it."

"When was this?"

"Right after the funeral. The next day, in fact. I thought it was kind of strange, but then I didn't say anything. I just did as she told me to do."

"Do you have the file on this case?"

"Yes. But it's in Mr. Norton's private file," she pointed to a small three-drawer file, "over there."

Rock gave it a quick glance. Why the devil would Stan have a locked file in his office? He'd never known him to take any cases which would have anything more slanderous in it than a divorce case.

"Do you know where he kept the keys?"

"On his key ring, along with the office key and his car keys. I suppose Mrs. Norton has those things now."

"Perhaps. Or the police."

The girl looked at Rock. A strange expression crossed her face, briefly, almost unnoticeable but Rock caught it.

"Do you know anything about the Jeffries case that I should know? Anything that I haven't been told?"

"I don't know what you've been told, Mr. Harris. But, if you want my opinion, I think there is something going on that would be pretty bad if it ever came out. I think that's why Mrs. Norton wanted to settle out of court when she knew that Mr. Norton would not defend her."

"Mr. Norton would never do a dishonest thing," Rock stated flatly.

"The Mr. Norton you knew ceased to exist over a year

89

ago. Mr. Harris." The girl spoke softly, as though she hated to say the words.

"Just exactly what are you insinuating, Miss McCormick?"

She tried to explain.

"It was just about a year ago when those special-delivery letters began to arrive here at the office. They didn't come at any regular time. We never knew when to expect one.

It was shortly after that Mr. Norton bought the small set of files to which only he had the key. And, in the last month, there was an increase of special delivery letters. Each letter seemed to age Mr. Norton ten years.

"Do you know who they were from?"

"No. There must have been more than one person because there was different handwriting."

"How many different ones would you say?"

"Golly, I don't remember. Maybe ten or twelve."

"But they all came special delivery?"

"Yes."

Rock stirred the papers on the desk. "Was there a Jeffries file? I couldn't find it in the cabinet."

"Yes. There was one. But Mr. Norton decided, just before he died, that he would not handle the case. He mentioned it to me. I wondered why at the time." She looked longingly at the door. "May I go now?"

"Of course." Rock stood up as she rose to leave. "And thank you for your help, Miss McCormick."

"Help? I'm afraid I couldn't tell you very much."

"You told me more than you realize."

He sat down again as the girl left the office.

*What happened to the Jeffries file?* he thought. *If I could only get into that locked file, maybe I could get a lead on this whole mess. Who has those keys? Maybe that*

*file is in the stuff that the police took with them, the pa-*
*pers from the desk. Maybe that was what he was working*
*on. Would the police let me have a look at the papers?*
*Only one way to find out.*

He picked up the phone and dialed the police station.

"Sergeant Lempinen."

"This is Rock Harris. How are you Dale?"

"Well hi there, Rock. Pretty good, pretty good. And
you?"

"Okay, Dale." Rock plunged right in with his question.
"I was wondering whether I could see those papers that
the police took off Stan Norton's desk, Dale. I think there
might be some case-stuff in there that I need. I'm at Stan's
office, now, trying to straighten out some of the mess."

"I don't know. Just a minute."

Rock could hear him drop the receiver on the desk and
scrape his chair back. He could hear him when he called
"Chief! Rock Harris wants to look at those papers we took
from Norton's place. Is it okay?"

Rock couldn't hear the chief's answer but in a moment
the sergeant picked up the phone again. "He says okay.
But they have to stay here."

"Good. I just want to go through them and see if any
of the stuff that's missing here is in that batch of papers.
Be right down."

"Okay. See ya'." The two receivers clicked simultaneous-
ly.

As he left the office he said, "If anyone calls, I'll be
back in a few minutes. I'm going down to the police station."

The girl nodded and smiled and kept on typing.

It was only a short walk. People spoke to Rock on the
street, people he knew and some he remembered by face

91

but not by name. Of course there were many newcomers whom he did not recognize but as he passed offices and stores with big windows, he was surprised at all the people he did know. It gave a good feeling to be recognized to be spoken to. For such a long time, as he'd wandered, every face had been a strange one. In foreign countries the smiles were rare indeed, and never on a face one knew. Those faces, in most instances, were gaunt and hollowed by hunger, etched by fear, and discouraged by life. He could not help but compare the faces along Ludington street with others he'd seen before he returned to America. He reached the police station and hurried up the steps.

Corporal Clark, whom he remembered only slightly, sat at the outer desk giving an eye test for a drivers license. Evidently he remembered Rock, or expected him, because he said, "Go right in. Sergeant Lempinen is waiting for you." Rock swung the outer gate open and walked through into the inner office marked Chief. Sergeant Lempinen sat at a desk across the room.

"Well hello, Rock. Sure has been a long time!" The sergeant rose and shook Rock's hand vigorously. "Sit down. Take a load off your mind." The Sergeant indicated a chair pulled up to the desk. "I brought the papers in here," he motioned to the neat stack on his desk, "sure too bad about Stan."

Rock sat down. "I miss him, Dale." He looked around the office. "Last time I was in town you were pounding a beat, weren't you? Or were you collecting pennies and nickles from the meters?" Rock laughed.

"I think I was pounding the beat — that's a few years ago," the Sergeant laughed as Rock took the stack of papers from him and began to thumb through them. He pushed away from the desk and added, "You can take your time. No one will bother you in here."

"Thanks, Dale. This shouldn't take long."

The papers seemed to be nothing more or less than a batch of briefs and outlines for some of the cases which had been scheduled for the next term of court. Stan, being the able lawyer he was, had more than his share of good cases. Of course there were some minor cases which eventually would be settled out of court, but the outlines were there, neat and legible and ready.

It took longer than Rock realized it would. He didn't know exactly what he was looking for but he knew that it would be something he could sense when he found it. Three quarters of the way through the pile he found the first piece of the puzzle. It was a plain piece of paper with a list of names on it. He ran his finger down the list. It seemed to be names of most of the prominent families in town. After several of them was a check mark in red. One of those marked was the name Jeffries. Rock pulled the paper out and read the list over again. Just what was this supposed to be, he thought. Names mean nothing in themselves, but with the red checkmark and especially when one of the names happens to be Jeffries — this could be what I'm looking for, he thought.

He studied the list a few minutes longer then put it aside and began to check the remaining papers. Toward the bottom he found another paper. This one made more sense to him. It was a brief of the Jeffries case, typed, but with added notes in the margins in Stan's handwriting.

He didn't hear the outer door open, nor did he hear Kari and Sergeant Lempinen when he ushered her in. The first he was aware of her was when she slid her cool hands over his eyes and snuggled her nose in his hair.

"Almost through?" she asked.

He pulled her hands down and pulled her to him as he turned around. "You scared me, baby."

"Did you find anything?"

"I think so."

"What?"

"Several pieces of a puzzle which do not fit together — at least in my mind."

"Like what?"

"Like a list of names, and a brief of the Jeffries case." He frowned. "Somehow I'm positive they must be the leads I'm looking for."

"Can you take them out?"

"No. This is evidence. It has to stay here."

"Evidence."

"Yes. Until the case is settled, this stuff has to stay here."

"Can't you copy it?"

"Yes." Rock yelled for the Sergeant.

"Yeah?" What can I do for you?" Sergeant Lempinen's head popped around the door and his grin was infectious.

"Can I borrow some paper? I want to write a few names down."

"Sure." The head disappeared only to reappear shortly with some notepaper. "This do?" he asked.

"That's fine. Thanks, Dale."

Sergeant Lampinen winked at Kari. "It pays to keep these guys happy. Especially my pal here."

Kari smiled at him, but said nothing. She was much too concerned with Rock, with the list of names, and with the actions of Mac as she left the house to meet Rock.

She mentioned none of these things until Rock had

finished with the papers and they were on their way out of the police station.

At the bottom of the steps, in full view of anyone who might be watching, Rock pulled her to him and kissed her with tender passion. Only the sharp whistle of a passing newsboy on his bike brought them both back to the time and place. Rock laughed and Kari blushed as they hurried down the street.

"What was that for?" Kari asked.

"For being a good girl!"

"Oh." Then her grin matched his.

"Why didn't Mac come with you? I thought she had some shopping to do?" Rock's sudden question brought Kari down to earth.

"She was going to, then decided not to. She said she expected a caller. I don't know whether she meant in person or a phone call. Bengy was there for a while and left just before I did." Kari looked up into Rock's face. "I think Bengy is sick," she said.

"Aw — he's just love sick." Rock said. "He's been mooning over Mac for as long as I can remember. Since she was in Beauty School."

"Poor man." Kari said.

"Poor fool!"

Kari looked up briefly. "You know, there — but for the grace of God —" she began the quote but Rock interrupted.

"Yeah," he said quietly.

They were in the second block when Rock nudged her gently and whispered, "Here comes one of the names on the list I found — Mrs. Langenford."

The woman approaching them was dressed in the height of fashion, plain but smart. Her smile was genuine and she stopped and held out her hand to Rock.

95

"It's nice seeing you again, Rock. I'm glad you're here."

He shook her hand. "Roberta, you're looking stunning, as usual."

The woman smiled at Kari then. "You want to watch him, my dear, he always was the most charming flatterer in the crowd."

Kari grinned. "I'm glad to know these things. It will prepare me for any emergency."

"Will you be here long?" Mrs. Langenford asked Rock.

"Not any longer than I can help. I didn't plan on being here now.

She hesitated a moment then said, "I'd like to talk to you before you leave, — on business."

"Was Stan handling anything for you?" Rock asked.

She looked at him with a strange expression on her face. "Why — yes. He had some unfinished business . . ."

"Rock nodded. "I found your name in his papers. Will you be free tomorrow?"

"Yes."

"Good. How about two o'clock? In Stan's office?"

"Fine. I'll be there." She turned to Kari then. "Get him out of this town as fast as possible, Miss Brent. And bless you both —" she added.

They walked on. Kari deep in thought as she repeated the remark to herself and Rock, a frown on his face.

Kari shuddered. The warning again.

# CHAPTER THIRTEEN

MAC SAT AT the desk in the library. Stan's desk. It was too neat now, and Mac looked out of place behind it. Her highly-polished nails beating a rapid tattoo on the hand-rubbed finish sounded like a muffled, off-beat machine gun. Mac was nervous. Her violet eyes were narrowed and she kept biting at her upper lip, a gesture she'd held over from leaner days. Her suit a peculiar shade of rust that just matched her hair, fit her lithe shape without a fraction of waste material. A diamond bracelet, sparkled and matched her tiny diamond earrings.

Why didn't the phone ring? She'd been waiting for a call from the girl at the office. She was supposed to let Mac know when one of the special delivery letters arrived at the office. And today was the day for one of them to be delivered.

When the phone did ring, at exactly 2:34, she jumped to her feet and stood there — unable to lift the phone. It rang five times before she put her hand out to pick up the receiver.

"Yes?"

"Mrs. Norton?" It was the girl from the office.

"Of course."

"There is a letter here for you — a special delivery letter."

"I'll send Bengy down after it. Give it to him."

"All right."

"He'll be right down."

"Yes." The girl hung up the receiver in Mac's ear.

"Damn little bitch," Mac muttered.

She placed the receiver back in its cradle and sat down again. Bengy should be here anytime. The last week she couldn't remember when he'd been sober. It was as though he couldn't stand himself, nor anyone else, including Mac. A few drinks seemed to relieve the pressure.

She heard the front door open. She relaxed in the chair and a tight smile curled the corner of her lips. This was the only indication of tension about her. She waited for him to appear.

The door opened slowly. Bengy was in no hurry to come in. He hesitated a moment before he appeared. The smile on Mac's lips grew tighter as she waited.

"What are you waiting for?" she could stand it no longer.

Bengy startled, stepped quickly into the room then and closed the door behind him. " 'Lo, Mac," he closed his eyes a moment and tried to stand very still. It didn't work.

"Well, it's about time you showed up. Where've you been?" she asked.

"Oh, around . . ." he answered, shrugging his shoulders.

"Christ! What a mess you are! You were supposed to

have been here a long time ago. You knew there'd be a letter to pick up at the office!"

"Sure! Sure! I'll pick up your letter. I'm all right. Just a couple drinks." Bengy wiped his mouth with the back of his hand.

"You're not fit to pick up anything! Including yourself!"

"Now Mac, don't get sore. I didn't do nothin' wrong. Just a couple of drinks. Jeez, this room gives me the creeps! How the hell can you sit there in Stan's chair?"

"It's easy. I've been thinking of it for a long time." Mac looked around the book-lined library. She coveted it and what it stood for and what it was. A quiet dignity about the room that Stan had loved, that he had given the room. — something she wanted more than anything else. A quiet dignity.

Bengy, plus scotch, became truthful. "It doesn't fit you, Mac, you don't suit the room."

"It fits me, it fits me perfectly!" Her eyes flashed a warning at him.

But Bengy was high. "Nope. You stick out like a bustle at a Japanese wedding. You're way out, Mac, darling." He chuckled as he squinted at her with one eye closed.

"You're drunk!"

"Yup. I'm drunk. Damn good and drunk! Feels good, too! First time I've felt good since you . . ." then he realized what he was about to say and it permeated the warmth of the haze which surrounded him.

"Since I what?" Mac's eyes were violet daggers. "Since I what, Bengy?" she purred softly.

"Oh hell, skip it will you, Mac? I didn't say nothin' — nothin' at all."

"Since I what Bengy?" she persisted.

He withered. "Since nothin'." He sagged into a chair and waited for the proverbial lash to fall.

"If you ever let that slip again, Bengy, I'll kill you!" Mac's voice was filled with fear for an instant. "Remember, I'll kill you!"

"How could I forget."

"Don't. It won't pay dividends. You can be sure of that."

Bengy looked up at her then. His bleary eyes watering for himself and for Mac. He started to cry.

Mac turned away from him, her anger gone. Her face was calm again. She hated tears. They reminded her too much of her childhood.

"For God's sake, shut up!"

But Bengy could no more control his tears than he could control Mac.

Mac paced back and forth in front of the desk.

"Shut up!" It was a hiss. It did the trick.

Bengy, startled at the closeness of her soft voice, jumped and pushed back in his chair. The sobs stopped. The curl came back to the corner of her lips, "someone might misunderstand. Do you hear? No more of this!"

Bengy nodded. "I'm sorry, Mac. Guess I had too much scotch."

"See that you don't do the same thing again."

"I won't."

"The trial came off all right. What have you got to worry about? You heard the verdict. Accidental death. Can't you get that through your head?"

"And it doesn't bother you?"

"No. Why shoud it?"

"I can't get it out of my mind. How can you?"

"I have. It's just as I planned it. You might as well make up your mind. There was never anything you could do about it anyway."

"How you can be so cold-blooded —"

"Maybe. But it's over. All over."

"But I can still see him trying to get his nitro —" Bengy shuddered.

"I don't want to hear this again, ever."

Bengy sighed, a long, drawn out sigh. He had spent himself, and now there were no more tears, no more feeling. Nothing.

"You'd better go get that letter."

"Yes." Bengy was sober.

She walked over to the window and looked out over the expanse of lawn, out across the bay. "Hurry." She also saw Paul romping with his dog McTavish near the hedge.

Bengy walked out without answering. He had no more answers for Mac. Scotch on the rocks had been his brief protest against what Mac had done. But even that had passed and there were no answers left.

Mac watched at the window until he was out of sight.

She returned to the desk and sat down, this time quietly. The tension was there but it was under control. Soon there would be another thousand dollars to add to her bank account. The women who had always snubbed her, had grown up with her, had known her, would not be able to turn from her, ever again. With her neat plan of fancy blackmail, she had quietly but devilishly, turned down the screws and the big pinch was on.

Her long range plan had begun to pay off. It had been paying off for over a year now. The bank account was fat, and getting fatter. It would soon be fifty-thousand dollars.

She was still sitting there when Bengy returned. She heard him come in and watched the door.

There was no expression on his face when he handed her the letter.

She smiled at the care with which the address had been printed. The person who had mailed it had been careful

101

not to leave any identifying handwriting on it. That had been one of the stipulations. All printed words, nothing else. Printed words and one thousand dollars. Her dark red nails ripped at the flap.

There was nothing inside except a note. It read:

If you think you can get any more money from me you'd better think again. It was a very interesting verdict. Accidental death?

The note was not signed. No trace of the sender was on it. Each letter was perfectly formed, as if a guide rule had been used. But Mac knew who'd sent it. Her face was white, her lips a straight, pinched line of scarlet. She crumpled the paper in her hand and slapped the desk top with the other. It was quick, sharp, like the snap of a whip. Bengy jumped, startled.

"Bitch!" she said, "bitch —"

"What's wrong?"

She made no answer.

"Hey —," Bengy leaned across the desk and took the crumpled paper from her hand, began to read aloud. "If you think you can get —" he stopped and looked at Mac now. "Do you think —?"

"I don't think. How could anyone know anything, especially her," she gave the note a brief glance, checked a number in the phone book and picked up the phone.

When the dial tone came through she dialed a number. It rang through three times and was answered. Mac hesitat for only an instant.

"You know who this is," she purred, her velvet voice low, silky.

The answer was cautious, almost inaudible. "Yes." A woman's voice said.

"I just got your letter."

"Yes."

"You made a mistake."

"No."

"Oh, but you did. Things haven't changed. I still can go to your husband.

"I don't think you'll go to anyone's husband." The woman's voice was flat, without inflection.

Mac's face was deadly white with frustration. "You won't have another chance. I'm not fooling."

"No. You don't fool. That was evident at the inquest."

These words were sharp. Mac sucked in a quick breath. "What do you mean by that?"

"You know what I mean. Rock Harris was not satisfied. And the coroner's verdict — accidental death."

"What do you mean?"

"I mean that Rock Harris is doing a good job. It's nice to have a friend like him. Your husband was his friend. He's not satisfied with the answers."

"The case is closed." Mac said.

"Some don't think so. I'll take a chance." The receiver clicked into place at the other end of the line.

Mac sat down abruptly. Bengy watched her in fascination. He'd heard the conversation and was aware of all it implied. That death was not accidental. That Stan could have been alive today.

Mac thought nothing of these things. To her, the disappointment of the brief note with no money was primary. She thought nothing of the implications, the insinuations, all she could think of was the fact that one of her steady donors had refused to pay her.

She had been swindled out of a thousand dollars. She had expected one thousand more dollars to put in her account. She had been refused, her threats ignored. It would serve the bitch right if she would take her information to the woman's husband. It would serve her right. But what could she gain by it? Would this further her program or would it start a chain reaction? She slid back in her chair. It was a large, easy chair, one that Stan had ordered especially made for himself. It was much too large for Mac, and she seemed, for a moment, lost and forlorn.

"It's not worth the risk," her voice had a note of dispair in it now. Her coat of armor had just received a blow, one that she had not anticipated.

"Why wasn't I born rich, Bengy?" For a moment she was a little girl again. "Why do I have to struggle?"

"You don't have to struggle." He came to her side and took her face in his hands and tilted it back so that she could look into his face. "We don't need any of this, Mac. Let's put this behind us. It isn't worth the price. We can go away. They'll soon forget us. We can make a whole new life, you and me. And Paul. He would like that, Mac. So would I."

She almost responded. She looked into his face and read the love mirrored there. Love for her. And she knew sorrow for the first time. And she turned away from it. It was an emotion she couldn't understand. She closed her eyes and pulled her face from his hands.

"I'm sorry, Bengy. I am truly sorry. I wish I could go away with you. But inside I would always be the same. It would ruin us. We would be miserable.

Bengy turned from her then and walked away. "Yes. I understand. I should have known better than to ask such a thing of you." He stood at the window and looked out over the lake. "God help you, Mac."

Her face was inscrutable. For a brief moment she had stepped out of character and allowed an inner small voice to speak. She went back over the last two weeks bit by bit to see where she might have erred. There was nothing

She had carefully protected herself every bit of the way. How dare Rock come back and upset her plan for the future. Of course she could kill Rock. There would be some way. And Kari. She'd started the whole thing with some of her answers. But there would be some way to turn Rock off the track. She could do that. After all, he and Kari were the ones who found Stan. He could be framed somehow. She could fix that.

"Don't feel sorry, Bengy," she said finally. "I can always start up the flame with Rock again."

"Don't over estimate yourself, Mac."

She smiled. "He still can be had."

"Don't be too sure. He has Kari now."

"Damn Kari." Her voice was velvet now. "I can handle her."

Bengy knew the menace of this voice.

# CHAPTER FOURTEEN

Wesley Bjornquist was coming out of the library as Kari came downstairs from her room. She had taken a nap after lunch and Rock had said he'd be back about 2:30. It was almost that now.

The sheriff paused as she reached the bottom of the stairs. "Is there someplace where we can talk, Miss Brent?"

Surprised, Kari motioned to the living room. "I suppose we can talk in here," she said.

"Good." The sheriff stood aside to let her pass.

"I've told you everything I know," she said as she passed him. He followed her into the room and waited until she had seated herself. Without preliminaries he pulled a chair closer and sat down.

"I am not here to question you, Miss Brent. Had some other business to finish. Nothing to be alarmed about. I'd like to ask a few questions about Rock. He's got nothing to hide, has he?"

"Of course not. But I can't see what good it is going over all this same routine so many times. Are you trying to see if I've made all this up and maybe might forget the answers? I have told you everything I know."

"Have you known Rock Harris long, Miss Brent?"

"About eight months. Why?"

"Only eight months. And you've been engaged for how long?"

"I don't see what that has to do with it?"

"Please. For how long —?"

"Two months."

"I see. And during this time were you together a great deal?"

"No. I was called home."

The sheriff stopped her then. "I know. You don't have to go into that. I'm sorry." He pushed his chair away from her a bit and leaned back. His next question was direct and to the point.

"How do you think Stanley Norton died?"

"Well —"

"How do you think he died?"

"I'm not sure. But, after talking to him that day, I'm positive he didn't kill himself either accidentally or on purpose. Mr. Norton was not a coward. He would not commit suicide. And how could it be an accident? This was not the first attack he'd had. But still —"

"You don't really think it was an accident, do you?" He watched her face closely.

"But if it wasn't an accident, it was —" she hesitated, "murder?"

"Yes. It could be murder."

"Deliberate murder?"

"Yes. Deliberate murder."

"But how?"

107

"I don't know. That's what I'm trying to find out. That's why I want you to remember everything. It might be important.

Kari did not answer. It could be, she thought . . . it just could be. But if it wasn't an accident, and he didn't do it himself, then who . . . who could want this fine man dead? Who would even think such an evil thought? Stanley Norton was one of the kindest, most gentle men Rock had ever known. And Kari had the same impression, even though she had only met him once.

Only one question was uppermost in her mind. "Who would do such a thing? Why — how?"

"Yes. That's what I'd like to know. How? That's what has me stumped at this point. How it was done. Logically, there's only one way it could be done. You couldn't get in the door, so the house was locked. They boy was up in his room and he saw and heard — but what did he see and hear? We know he saw you and Rock arrive. We know he saw Mac and Bengy leave the house. You, actually, and Rock were the only two people around."

"That's ridiculous. Paul couldn't possibly have seen everything. His room faces the front and he could only see in that direction and as far as the angle would permit. Someone could have come from the back. After all, if someone planned this they wouldn't have come up the front walk!" Kari was indignant.

"No. You have a point there. But the house was still locked. How do you account for that?"

"I don't account fo any of it. I only know that Rock and I had to find a way in. He was not away from me long enough to do anything. And, no matter what happened before, Rock liked Stan. He was like a father to him. He would have protected him."

"Men do strange things to protect those they love."

108

"Rock did not kill Stan, Mr. Bjornquist."

"The house was locked. You were the only ones inside."

"Someone could have gone in the same way we did."

"Rock seemed to know the way pretty well."

"Rock should. He was brought up here. There must be others who know how to get in. He wouldn't be the only one —"

"Perhaps not. But the boy saw no one else, heard no one else. And — Rock's fingerprints were all over the library. Only Rock's prints. The room had been cleaned thoroughly that afternoon. Cleaned and polished by the maid. His were the only prints we found. His and Stan's."

"Naturally. I was there too. But someone else could have worn gloves."

"They could have. But none of Rock's prints were smeared or smudged. They were fresh."

"Stan may have had someone else in here before we came. They could have had an appointment. He could have let them in himself."

"His prints were not on any of the doorknobs. Only Rock's. Evidently when he came in the doors must have been open."

"He could have let them in the back way."

"No caller would come in the back way. And Paul would have heard them in the library. He heard everyone else." The sheriff paused. "He didn't see or hear anyone else."

"Whoever it was could have been very quiet. After all, they were not eager to have anyone know they were there. They must have worn gloves, too."

"All right. Saying that all this is true. That someone came in, unseen. What about the drink? Stan had a drink with someone. He wouldn't have offered a drink to anyone except a friend."

109

"No. But then again, he wasn't supposed to drink. The doctor was very emphatic about that. He said that Stan never drank. Never. He didn't touch a drop."

Wesley Bjornquist nodded briefly. "This is not general knowledge. But the lab tested the clothing he was wearing. Those damp spots on his suit were liquor with a weak test of nitro."

Kari gasped. "The nitro?"

"Yes. So you see he did have some nitro. But what happened to it? Where was it? Did he put it in his drink?"

"But I understood that they were little pills?"

"They were. Then how did they get in his drink?"

Kari shook her head. This was a new bit of information. How could the nitro have gotten in the liquor. And, if Stan never drank, why did he drink this particular evening? He would have taken the pill orally. He never would have diluted it in his drink. He was too smart to have done anything that stupid. What had happened? Everyone else at the inquest had had a good alibi, had witnesses, had proof that they had been elsewhere. Everyone except Rock and her. And the sheriff was positive now that Stan had been murdered. She knew he thought that. He hadn't said murder. But Stan was dead. It was not by accident. It was not suicide. It must be furder. And she and Rock were the last ones with Stan.

"I don't see what could have happened. It's obvious that Mr. Norton talked with someone."

"Yes. He must have talked with him. But beyond that, he must have let him in the front door. He must have been with him in the library. They must have talked. Stan must have mixed a drink, or the man might have mixed it. Stan probably took it to be hospitable, even though he was not supposed to have any liquor. He could have had an attack while the man was there and probably reached for his nitro pills. The man, seeing this, must have taken them from him and put them in the drink to dilute them. Then he must have panicked and tried to give him some of the drink. It spilled and was too weak to do any good. He could have let himself out in time to meet you. He could have done all this — then made you think he'd just arrived."

Am I hearing right, Kari thought. Does he think Rock did this?

Wesley Bjornquist continued. "I hate to suggest these things, Miss Brent, but Rock has always been a strong willed person. It is possible that he killed Stan. Remember, they had not been on the best of terms for a long time."

"That was over and done with a long time ago. It was a silly thing to begin with, but at the time it seemed very important. Rock did not kill Stan."

"I have a letter from Rock to Stan that could very easily disprove your statement."

"You mean that letter he wrote when he learned Mac was going to marry Stan?"

Bjornquist nodded.

"Mac is just trying to put Rock into something so she can gloat. And she would like nothing better than to cause trouble between us. Rock wrote that letter after he got the "Dear John" letter from Mac. That was a long time ago. He's had time to learn that he was wrong. It wasn't Stan who was at fault. It was Mac. She wanted money and power. Rock had none of this. Stanley Norton had both. If she married Stan she would automatically become one of the upper set, people could no longer snub her. Now she wants to make more trouble — between Rock and me."

"She's only trying to find out what happened to her husband."

"I'd bet on that." Kari was angry now. What was this

man trying to get out of her? Did he think she would agree with him.

"She's been very nice to both you and Mr. Harris," Bjornquist said. "She invited you to stay here at her home. If she were trying to do anything to harm either of you, I don't think she would keep you in her home."

"No," Kari spoke sharply. "She only keeps us here to flaunt herself at Rock in front of me. She wants to keep track of what he's doing at the office. There is something she doesn't want him to find out. Rock did not kill Stan."

"Everything fits perfectly. Timing, clues, alibi, everything. He planned it well. There just isn't any other explanation."

"You're wrong. Rock had no reason to kill Stan. He wanted only to be friends again. I know Stan was looking forward to seeing Rock. I talked with him that afternoon. There was deep affection in his attitude when we spoke of Rock. Rock had no reason to kill Stan."

"Rock is a lucky man to have such a champion, Miss Brent."

"What do you mean by that?"

"I mean that if it weren't for you, Rock Harris would be charged with the murder of Stan Norton."

"You're not serious?"

"Yes. I would have put him in jail by now."

"But how can you? There's no evidence?"

"Everything says that Rock did it. There is a motive. The child saw no one else —"  -

"Then I'm glad I know differently. Rock is innocent."

"I don't go along with that."

Kari was not sure what he meant by the implication. She waited for him to elaborate. He said nothing else.

"Are you telling me all these things so that I'll run to Rock with it?" Kari asked.

"No, I'm trying to piece together certain facts."

"But you know I'll tell Rock."

"I would expect that."

"And Mac, what about Mac?"

"What about Mac?"

"She can't scare Rock. He won't scare. He knows there's something going on. He's trying to find it. But, I know him. You won't scare him with insinuations. Because, Mr. Bjornquist, Rock did not kill his best friend!"

Bjornquist sighed and shook his head slowly. "I wanted to talk to you, Miss Brent. You are his fiancee. If a man is suspected of a crime, especially murder, I think he should be aware of it. I talked with him this morning. He was very short with me. As if he were trying to hide something. Said he had a lot to do. Told me to go peddle my papers. But I have a job to do and I aim to do it to the best of my ability. I've never had to accuse a man of murder before. Before I go that far, I want all the facts. I want to know I'm right. Only you can help him by giving every fact — every little thing. You may know something you may not think important enough to tell."

"But I've told you everything — I know nothing more."

"I hope you're wrong. I hope you can remember something — some little thing — that will help prove his innocence.

"You mean —?"

"Yes. A murder charge."


Kari sat quietly while the sheriff let himself out. He was gone now. He thought Rock had killed Stan. He had been piling up evidence. It was strong against Rock. As angry as she was to think that Bjornquist entertained all these doubts since the inquest without anyone's knowing, she couldn't help admiring him for not arresting Rock before now. If it had been anyone else on the force, Rock would have been sitting in jail. Wesley Bjornquist had the reputation of being a fair and just man. He had the admiration of the entire town.

Kari walked to the window and looked out across the bay, without seeing any of the beauty. Several foreign yachts were tied up at the concrete dock along the yacht basin and small skiffs and gulls hurried over the water pushed by a south-east wind. It was bustling with activity as each boat on the bay cut through the choppy water and headed for their moorings. It was obvious to her that Bjornquist had a crush on Mac. She had watched him at the inquest. He, as many others did, kept their eyes on MacAllister. Kari knew it was a very good act but she hadn't realized until now that Mac had the men of town wrapped around her little finger. With her beauty, she created in the male animal a desire to fight for her, to win favor with her. It was obvious too, that it would take a great deal to pull him from the trail he had started. The trail which led to the arrest of Rock.

Kari knew how Rock felt about the murder. He couldn't understand how anyone could kill Stan, how they could walk in — either admitted by Stan or however they did get in — talk with Stan, for certainly there had been no struggle, kill him, then walk out without leaving some sort of trace. He knew how Bjornquist felt about Mac-Allister, he had once been a helpless pawn in the Mac-Allister game too. But he didn't realize that Bjornquist was trying to prove that he murdered his friend.

Kari knew it now. She knew what a dangerous man Wesley Bjornquist could be. Especially since he was collecting all these bits and pieces of evidence which pointed out Rock. Circumstantial evidence, but she knew that many men had been convicted on circumstantial evidence before, and many would be again. She didn't want Rock to be one of them. But she knew now that Mac would stop at nothing.

It always came around to Mac. A chill settled over Kari and she moved away from the window to pace back and forth in the library. Somehow this house was getting on her nerves. No matter where she turned, what she did, Mac always seemed to be somewhere in the vicinity. There always seemed to be so many things Rock must do for her. Kari was beginning to hate the sight of Mac. She was everywhere in this big, old house. Kari was homesick for the apartment in the city. Where she and Rock had spent only a few hours. The apartment of beautiful memories.

In this huge structure, the presence of MacAllister dominated every nook and cranny, every room, so that Kari felt unwanted, an alien presence. She could hear Mac's voice no matter where she went. It was velvet venom. And it injected itself into every conversation, every moment with Rock. It separated them.

She must get hold of herself. Wesley Bjornquist had filled her with doubts and fears. Not that Rock was a murderer, but doubts that could not be dispelled by mere words. She knew he was innocent of the crime. So how could they think he was the murderer?

But who had killed Stan Norton? If he had not died by accident, and had not commited suicide, then who had killed him? Everything pointed to Rock. It seemed that he was the only one who had had the opportunity.

Kari left the library. She had to get out of the atmosphere. She closed the door and walked aimlessly through the hall. One of the doors was partway open. She looked in. A back room, evidently used as a storeroom for things

**115**

that MacAllister did not want around. Things that obviously were Stan's things. Pictures of the family. Several hunting trophies, two deer heads and a moose head, a locked gun rack with five guns under glass. Kari walked up to the lovely, hand rubbed, oak piece. Three of the guns were modern, guns she understood and had used herself. One was a Winchester long rifle, one a double barrel shot gun and the other an automatic hammerless. The other two guns of ancient vintage, museum pieces.

Back in the corner stood a covered object, tall and slender. It looked like a harp. She remembered that Rock had mentioned that Stan used to play the harp. Kidded about it, in fact. This must be it. Did she dare look at it?

Carefully she uncovered the lovely object and gasped when it stood before her in it's graceful beauty. She touched the strings gently, awed by the tone. She stroked them, experimenting with variations. Even the discords and odd notes sounded beautiful to her. How could Mac hide this lovely thing away where it could not be played and heard, and seen. She forgot where she was and tried to find a melody. Her piano training helped and suddenly she found the pattern of the strings. Haltingly, she picked out an old favorite, lost in the sounds she was creating.

She didn't know when Stan's son came into the room to stand slightly behind her, at her side. But when she turned he stood there, rapt and enchanted, as she was, with the lovely strains. His face was intent and his eyes were almost closed. It was the first time she'd seen him with an expression of love on his face. The child was a picture, a miniature Stanley Norton. She had never noticed it before. His face had always been a tense, frightened mask, resembling no one but himself. Her fingers left the strings and his eyes opened wide into her's.

"Don't stop. Please! Oh, don't stop." he spoke softly.

"It is lovely, isn't it," Kari touched the strings again.

"Yes. I love it. Father —" his voice was silent, then he went on, "Father was teaching me to play —"

"He must have played it beautifully."

"Oh, he did. We used to play every evening. Until —"

Kari broke in. "Would you like to play for me? I have never played one before, but it's fascinating."

Paul had a warm glow on his face as he moved toward the huge instrument. Kari had never seen such a complete change in anyone. He stood with his shoulder and face cradling the polished wood as his fingers paused over the strings. Then he began. The music he played was simple, but he stroked the strings with a sureness for the right chords. Stan had loved the instrument. Now it brought Paul closer to his father. He had forgotten she was there.

One song ran into another and they both forgot time. Kari wondered, as she stood there nearby, how she could have missed this wonderful trait in Paul. He was no longer unsure, frightened, and afraid. She could feel the love for his father in every note he played, the expression on his face, his very stance at the instrument.

"Paul," she said softly, "the day your father died — are you sure you saw no one else . . . heard no one else? Only Rock and me?"

"There was no one else. Only you two —" he paused, "no one came in . . ."

"But could you have heard — could you have seen anyone?"

"I heard everyone. I saw —" he hesitated, "I could see everyone —"

"But didn't you turn away just a little?"

"Yes. But I could still see —!"

117

"But if you turned away — how could you always see?"

"Well I did. I saw everything."

"Won't you tell me —?" Kari pleaded.

Paul shook his head. "No. But I saw."

Kari knew he was telling the truth. She also felt that Paul knew something, something he had not told at the inquest.

"There's something you're not telling, Paul," she said, "dont' you trust me? Can't you tell me what it is you're hiding? I must know the truth."

He shook his head. "No. I can't."

"Why can't you tell me?"

"If I tell —" he began, then horror took the place of love in the boy's face. It startled Kari. The change was so abrupt, so overwhelming, that for an instant, she couldn't believe she actually had witnessed it. He tried to say words but they seemed frozen in his throat. Then they came out in a whisper, "I didn't say anything. I didn't say anything!"

Kari turned. MacAllister stood in the doorway of the room. On her face was an expression of hate, of violence. "You little brat!" she whispered in her soft, velvet voice. It made the hair stand up on the back of Kari's neck. Mac was approaching now, her eyes, two slits. Paul shrank back against Kari and she automatically put her arms around him. "How many times have I warned you to stay away from the harp!"

Kari could feel the boy shiver and a deep whimper escaped from his lips. She thrust out a protecting hand in front of Paul. "Mrs. Norton!" her voice was sharp. It broke the spell. MacAllister relaxed, her fingers flexed and she realized that Paul had a friend in Kari Brent.

"We'll talk about this later, Paul. Stay in your room

until I call you. And —" she emphasized the next words coldly, "stay out of here. Stay away from the harp."

Paul had not waited to hear. He had darted past her and raced up the stairway. The sound of the door of his room slamming came to them shortly.

Mac turned on Kari then. "While you are a guest in my home you can at least act like one." The menace was back in her voice again, "stay away from Paul. He's a very impressionable child — you only upset him with all your talk." She turned on her heel and walked to the bottom of the stairway. Kari thought she was going to go upstairs but she passed by and went into the library, slamming the door behind her.

Kari's thoughts were chaotic as she watched this new act. I've been wrong about Paul all along. He's so frightened of MacAllister that he can't even think. She doesn't deserve a fine boy like Paul. I'll never forget the look on his face — like a very small, terrified animal — so terrified no one could ever get him to say anything about the trial, about Stan, about anything.

She couldn't talk to Paul any more. Of this she was sure. His stepmother's threats must have been vicious to have frightened him like that. Kari wondered what she had said to him. She would have to try to find out from some other source. She must try.

Kari looked around the small room, then closed the door behind her, almost bumping into Bengy in the hall. He jumped at her appearance and, when she motioned to him that she wanted to talk to him, he hesitated, then motioned to the stairway.

Mac and Bengy had been talking in the library when Mac heard the music. Kari had made no effort to be quiet.

119

Bengy hurried past the closed library door. Kari walked to the end of the hallway where they could converse without danger of being interrupted or heard.

"I didn't know that playing the harp was forbidden around here," she began. "Paul loves the instrument. He heard me playing it. He couldn't resist and came in — what's this all about?"

"I'm sure I don't know what's gotten into Mac. That's Stan's harp — maybe she can't stand the sound of it yet." Bengy answered, floundering around for words.

"It positively transformed the child. He's a sensitive, very wonderful boy. But he's frightened."

"Frightened?"

"Yes. He was terrified when he saw Mac in the doorway. I never saw such a change in my life."

Bengy shrugged, "I don't know." Then he looked at her. "Did you talk about anything?"

Kari reddened. "Yes. The sheriff was here. I only asked Paul something the sheriff was trying to find out."

Why hadn't she told him exactly what she'd asked Paul.

Bengy had not given her any reason to distrust him, in fact she felt sorry for him, and pitied him. When he was not with MacAllister he was a different person. His Italian temperment was warm and friendly, and Kari enjoyed his companionship. Actually, he was around the house more than Rock had been since the inquest and she'd had the opportunity to get to know him better.

Kari was sure he felt the same way toward her. And she knew that he loved Paul, and now she knew he pitied him. She could see it in his face.

"I'll do my best," he said.

"She won't listen."

"Not Mac. I meant with Paul. I can talk to him. He likes me."

"I think I'll get some fresh air. I could use some."

"Yes. Might be a good idea. Stay out of Mac's sight for a while. At least till she gets over —" Bengy stopped then realizing he was about to say something better left unsaid.

Kari knew what he meant. She nodded and watched him disappear into Paul's room. She wondered why Bengy had been so cautious. Was he hiding something? What did he know that he hadn't told at the inquest? Or was he just afraid of MacAllister? She realized now just how vindictive Mac could be. She shuddered again when she remembered the terrible look in Mac's eyes as she looked at the harp — then at Paul. She still could hear the fright in the small boy's voice. Suddenly the room seemed too filled with hate and fear and Kari wanted to get away.

Throwing her sweater around her shoulders she hurried out the front door and down across the Shore Drive into the lake front park. The fresh air brought a measure of relief as she walked along the shoreline. It was almost dark now. Boats were beginning to tie up for the night. The larger boats with more draft anchored offshore and rocked gently behind the protection of the man made peninsula, the jutting finger that calmed the waves as they rolled shoreward from the wide expanse of Lake Michigan proper.

She tried to recall all the points the sheriff had brought out. Before she realized how far she'd walked she stumbled over the rubble of the rock and driftwood-strewn beach at the far end of the park. It was dark now and a fog was drifting in. She shivered in the dampness and turned toward the lights of town.

Intent on picking her way back through the littered

121

beach, she was not aware of anyone behind her until there was a stumble over some loose rock and the noise reached her. She hurried along in the soft sand. She could not hear the footsteps of her pursuer. It seemed to be staying about twenty paces behind her. In the thick fog it was hard to tell whether or not it was a man.

Kari reached the whiteness of the concrete retainer wall and hesitated. She turned suddenly and was not sure that something wasn't moving behind her. The hairs on the back of her neck stood out. She could sense a presence that she couldn't see. It was too dark. And the fog was much too thick. Silly, she thought. You're getting the jitters. There's no one there.

She began to walk rapidly again, along the breakwater. Why did she feel that there were moving shadows behind her? She didn't hear any footsteps. This was certainly getting her down. She'd be glad when Rock was through at the office — through checking Stan's papers for Mac. It would be good to get away from this town, get away with Rock.

She paused at the edge of the concrete, relieved that she was almost up to the first yacht. She could just see it's form moving gently on the swells. No one seemed to be aboard. Everything was dark.

Then it happened. Before she could cry out, she felt two hands push against her back and send her stumbling into the darkness of the water. Kari went down, the chill water of Lake Michigan closed over her head and she held her breath. The suddenness of her plunge carried her several feet under and she kicked her feet to propel herself upward. An expert swimmer, she felt no alarm at being in the water. She felt more alarm at who might be still waiting for her at the dock's edge. Someone had tried to kill her. Someone who perhaps was hoping she couldn't swim.

She tred water silently, making no more motion than she had to to keep upright in the cold water. Whoever it was was making no effort to come to her aid. She could see nothing. Nothing except the swirling clouds of fog. She could hear nothing except the ripples as they hit the concrete base of the breakwater.

She was frightened. She couldn't stay here all night treading water. It was cold. There was a killer on the beach. She waited a long moment more, then swam silently toward the outline of the yacht. Whoever was on shore could not see her. If she couldn't see them, they certainly couldn't see her. The fog had become an ally, the fog and the black water.

The boat loomed big and white over her. One of the lines to the dock was slack and she held on to it to rest. Her clothes were heavy and her shoes were pulling her down. She waited and listened. Only the slap of water against the boat was audible. There were no other sounds. Cautiously she let go of the line and swam to the dock. With difficulty she pulled herself out of the water and hugged the cold concrete. She wanted to make herself as inconspicuous as possible. But there were no sounds.

She knew then that this first boat was tied up almost directly in front of MacAllister's home, across the park and directly in line of sight with the front windows. She was grateful for the fog now as she left the concrete pier and made her way up across the park, across the Lake Shore Drive and up across the huge, lighted porch.

Before she reached the door it was thrown open and Rock came running out.

"For God's sake what happened to you?" he pulled

123

her through the door, dripping, shivering, and picked her up in his arms.

"Someone pushed me in the yacht basin." Kari explained through chattering teeth.

"They what?" Rock almost exploded.

"Do you think I'd go for a swim in the fog — in all my clothes?"

"I wouldn't be surprised." MacAllister's voice purred from the library doorway.

Kari shivered again. But Rock's arms held her tightly to him and she slid her arms around his neck. She felt safe now. Rock had her. No one could hurt her now. She looked over Rock's shoulder. MacAllister was watching them, her eyes half closed, Kari saw this. Then she noticed something else. Mac was wearing black. A long, black evening gown with a jacket. The jacket had long sleeves. It would have been impossible to see black through the fog. She would look like a shadow. Mac had seen her leave the house. She was positive now. She had seen her leave, had followed her and waited until she was sure she'd not be seen. Not seen by either Kari nor by anyone else.

But who would believe her. She had no proof. Except that she was sure. Rock was at the foot of the long stairway now, about to carry her upstairs. Mac's voice stopped him.

"Weren't you frightened?" She asked in the velvet tone that Kari knew so well.

Kari made no answer. Now she knew she was right. Mac had wanted to frighten her, kill her if possible, but to frighten her. There must be a great deal involved. She was getting too close to the answers to the puzzle. The puzzle that Rock was trying to put together. What was it that Mac was afraid she knew? She didn't recognize anything that could be dangerous to Mac.

# CHAPTER FIFTEEN

MAC WAS PACING back and forth in front of Stan's desk again, her face contorted with anger. She was seething within at Bengy, at Kari, and most of all at Rock. How dare he flaunt that little bitch in front of her. When Bengy opened the door and stepped in, she turned on him, almost catlike, ready to pounce. He stopped, startled at her fury.

"Have you done anything about that letter yet?" she spat out.

"Letter?"

"Oh, for the love of God, do you have to repeat like a parrot? The letter I got from —" she hesitated at mentioning the name — even in her own home.

Bengy's face was calm. He looked at her with what seemed to be almost pity.

"Well," Her eyes sparkled dangerously and she stood motionless, waiting for his answer.

"No."

"Why not?"

"I'm not sure I'll do anything about it. After all, there is nothing that says she has to do anything she's made up her mind not to do."

"Oh. Going soft on me?"

"No. Not soft, Mac. But —" he hesitated, "isn't there one spark of decency left? Are you really as hard and cruel as you seem?"

Mac snorted derisively. "Hard! Cruel! My dear Bengy, you've seen only a small sample of just how hard and cruel I really can be." Her voice lowered and took on the purring menace of a jungle cat. "They'll pay. They will pay whatever I ask."

Bengy again said the wrong thing, "How is Kari after her swim?"

"Kari! Kari! She's fine! Everyone thinks about Kari. Why doesn't anyone think about me?"

"I think about you, Mac, I think what wrong you are doing and it scares hell out of me. Where will all this end?"

"End? It will end when I get damn good and ready. I'll have money. Plenty of money. And power. They will never be able to snub me, to turn up their noses at me again."

"I think you've made a mountain out of a mole hill, Mac — people aren't as bad as you paint them."

"You don't know. Bengy, you really don't know how cruel people can be. And don't give me all that talk about them not knowing what they are doing."

"People do many things without realizing why they are doing them, Mac. There maybe many reasons. Habit," he ticked them off on his fingers, "anger, pressure — many reasons. But I think sometimes that habit is the biggest reason."

"I don't give a damn about reasons."

126

"I know — I know."

"I want results. And fast."

"I'm aware of that." Bengy sighed deeply. "I'm only trying to figure out why it is such a driving force with you."

Mac made no answer. She walked to the window and looked out. Her eyes narrowed as she saw Kari crossing the park in front of the house.

"Now what's she up to?" she whispered, almost inaudible.

But Bengy heard. "What's who up to?"

"That little bitch!" It was hard for Mac to say Kari's name. The overwhelming jealousy formed a block for her where Kari and Rock were concerned and stirred up emotions within her.

"Kari?" Bengy was beside her now, looking over her shoulder at the graceful figure of Kari headed for the concrete dock. Bengy hated what he was about to say. But Mac was not looking at him. "Mac."

She made no movement, no effort to answer.

His voice was harsh now. "Mac, what do you know about the accident?"

"Accident?"

"Yes. Last night. To Kari."

She turned then, slowly, pulling her attention away from the view of the beach. "Should I know anything about last night?"

"Did you push her in?"

It had been almost too easy. Dressed in black, she'd been invisible in the heavy fog. He could see the entire picture now and he shivered.

"Get hold of yourself, Bengy."

"You frighten me, Mac. I think I understand you better than anyone alive," he hesitated, "always have for that

127

matter, but when we watched Kari last night — from the window in the library — I didn't think you'd follow her and try to —" he stopped and looked at Mac, his eyes pleading with her to tell him he had it all wrong.

"Yes, Bengy. Try to what?" Her voice had the velvet texture again, smooth, silky and satanic.

But Bengy had his head in his hands, elbows on knees. "If only I didn't love you so much —" his whispered words ended in a sigh. "Why do you hate her Mac? She has done nothing to you." He was looking intently at her now. But Mac looked at him with pity.

"I don't know why you put yourself through all this torture, Bengy. It only makes you feel worse."

"I know it, Mac. But no matter what you do — even when I see you do it — it makes no difference."

Mac relaxed within herself again. She smiled at him with the secret smile he knew so well. The smile that could turn his every objection into a negative quantity. No matter what the argument, what the issue, he was again a man at her feet worshipping her, idolizing believing every word she chose to feed him. He had a sickness. And the sickness was Mac.

The thought of Rock brought her back to the problem. She spoke impatiently now, frowning as she turned to leave the room. "You'd better get on this letter thing. Write another. Really put the screws on this time. She can't go to the cops."

"But Mac —" Bengy protested. "She wasn't fooling, she'll go to the cops."

"I don't think so." Mac answered softly. "Just ask her if she thinks the scandal would be worth while — especially when her husband finds out that she's been playing around on the side."

"Maybe not, Mac. Maybe not."

"I don't think she'll gamble on that, Bengy."

As she closed the door behind her she could hear the click of the typewriter. Bengy was already at work. He would do a good job. She had him in line again. Perhaps this would be as good a time as any to go down to the office where Rock was still getting things in order. She wanted to see him anyway. After last night she wanted to see just what his reaction was to Kari's accident.

Her convertable stood in the drive and she backed it out swiftly. She drove as she did everything else, with ease, with sureness, with contempt. Her eyes flashed briefly across the shoreline as she drove past. Kari could not have seen a thing last night through that thick fog. Why even she had trouble keeping Kari in sight as she followed her, and she knew the beach like the inside of her hand. Any problems were always taken for a walk along the shore. The water, the sand, and the quiet, gave her more peace of mind than any other thing in the world.

Mac drove without regard for speed limit and drew up at the curb in front of the office in a matter of minutes. She glanced up to see if she could see any lights on in the office. But evidently there was no need for them yet. She hurried up the stairs and pushed the outer door open. The office girl was sitting at her desk working on some sort of form. She looked up when Mac came in.

"Oh. You startled me, Mrs. Norton. Good morning."

"Good morning." Mac was brief, "Is Rock here?"

"Yes. He's in Mr. Norton's office." She made a motion as if to get up and announce Mac.

But Mac waved her down with a quick gesture of annoyance. "Never mind. I know my way in." She pushed open the door to the inner office and walked in.

Rock sat at Stan's desk, a stack of papers in front of him, a pile of cigarette butts in the ash tray. He looked up, and waved vaguely to the chair beside his desk.

"Be with you in a minute, Mac," he said.

Mac's eyes snapped fire. She was not used to being practically ignored. She thought that Rock was still one of her stable and this casual manner was annoying. It hadn't been too many years back when Rock had been willing to die for her. He'd said so many times — in his youthful ardor. Her voice had always been able to pull him to her no matter how bad the quarrel had been. And now, here he was, sitting nonchalantly before her. Displaying in his manner, a new self dicipline, the result of his new professional status, his ability to stand on his two feet.

She squirmed a little in her chair, angry because Rock didn't turn to her and forget the work at hand. She pulled her dress up slowly to expose the long expanse of nylon covered leg. She had seen Rock admiring Kari's legs last night. She remembered when Rock had watched her legs with great admiration. She was sorry she hadn't made sure Kari wouldn't get out of the water last night. Maybe it was just as well, another death in such a short time would have been awkward.

She seethed within herself.

Then Rock pushed back his chair and grinned at her across the desk.

"I know it isn't polite to make a lady wait but I wanted to finish that before I lost it. I'm not too good at figures in the first place."

Mac relaxed now. She had the floor again. She slid her hand over the desk and covered his for a moment. It surprised him and the he slowly moved his hand out from ·under hers, his face reddening with embarrassment.

Mac laughed, a low, throaty laugh.

"Where's Kari?" he asked.

Irked by his ready question about Kari, Mac lowered her voice to it's most seductive pitch and answered. "She's all right. She's taking it easy. You've nothing to worry about."

Rocks smile disappeared as he answered. "I told her to go easy today. Last night's experience is enough to frighten anyone. Especially a girl who has never hurt anyone or anything in her whole life. Why anyone would want to hurt her is beyond me. I just wish she could have gotten a good look at whoever did it. She said it was too dark and the fog was too thick for her to see anything.

"Wesley said there was no trace of anything down there. He thought she might have imagined the whole thing." Mac's voice held a touch of amusement, sure that Rock would be less worrid if he knew Kari might have imagined it. Rock was busy with his thoughts and missed the implication that Mac had inferred. Mac realized that she had lost him again.

"Are you about finished here, Rock? Have you found anything out of order?"

Rock looked at her again. "Out of order?"

"Why — yes. I thought maybe there might be something that would need a lawyer . . . his advice."

"No. Stan's papers and cases were pretty much in order as far as I have been able to figure out. I am working on some of the income-tax papers now, getting them straightened out. Being administrator of a will is not always an easy job."

Mac smiled at him again. Stan had guarded well, the secret business she had been engaged in. He evidently had been shrewd enough not to leave any papers around that might incriminate himself or his wife. Of course there

131

was a chance that this was not the case, but Rock had been working here in the office for days now and had not found anything — at least he had said nothing to her about anything. And she knew him well enough to know that if he'd have found even the slightest trace, he would have come to her immediately.

"I'm sure it's not an easy job, Rock," she caressed him with her eyes. She knew that he was aware of it because his eyes watched her now. She relaxed. Stan was too smart too leave anything around. She remembered the first day one of the letters had been mailed to the office. Stan had not called her. He had come home with the letter. He had demanded an explanation. And she had given it to him.

Stan had been angry with Mac. He had warned her that he would not protect her in any way if she continued blackmailing her patrons. She had laughed at him. But she had not changed her mind. She had made him keep her letters at the office in a special file. Locked. And, after almost a year, Stan had turned against her. That was why it had been so easy to kill him. So easy. Now she was the very wealthy Mrs. Stanley Norton. Actually she didn't need the blackmail money — only the satisfaction of seeing the women squirm under her thumb. Squirm as they had made her squirm.

"You've been so busy that there hasn't been much time for anything." Mac said. "We've hardly had a chance to say more than a couple words to each other — about us."

Rock looked at her with raised eyebrows. "About us?"

"Yes, Rock, I know that you are sorry that you've become involved with Kari. But after all, isn't it better to find out now that you were never suited — than to marry and find it out later?"

"But how ridiculous can you get? Kari and I are going to be married. Mac, can't you understand that what we had between us is dead? Ever since you married Stanley. How do you figure that there could ever be anything between us now? After all, Stan was my best friend — your husband.

"Don't be so naive, Rock. You know that what we had was never dead, and now I'm more sure of it than before. Don't try to deny this."

Rock stared at her then. This was a side of Mac that he'd never been quite aware of before. After a long pause he spoke. "Isn't it a little strange that you are not mourning for Stan? You're so wrapped up in yourself that you have forgotten how to be a human being?"

"No, Rock. It's you who has forgotten." She must get him off this tack now, before he suspects something, she thought. "Rock . . . what is it you're trying to say?"

"I'm trying to find out why you have not mourned your husband, Mac."

Mac's heart stopped for an instant. He couldn't possibly suspect anything. He was just saying words. How could he suspect anything? She answered him carefully. "Rock, you don't think I wanted Stan to die?"

"No. I don't think that, Mac." His words were grave and he spoke then carefully, weighing each one before it was said. "He could have done so many things for you, Mac. So many things. And you've had a good life with him. No, I don't think you wanted him dead."

"I'm sorry." Rock stirred restlessly, wanting to get back to the work on the desk. He shuffled the papers.

"Then why this inquisition?"

Mac, angry at losing him again, spoke a bit sharply. "You're obviously anxious to get back to your work."

Rock knew now what her visit was for. He answered

shortly, almost curt. "I am in love with Kari, Mac. I want to finish this up as soon as possible. I've changed a great deal."

"You certainly have changed. But I haven't."

He looked at her intently. "No. I don't think you'll ever change, Mac. You always did have a set goal. I don't think anything or anyone will sway you from your path for long."

"Nor you from yours," Mac returned. "But that isn't why I came to talk to you. I came to warn you."

"Warn me? About what?"

"Didn't you realize that Wesley Bjornquist suspects that you know more than you told at the inquest? He even suspects that you may have quarreled with Stan that night —"

"Let's get this straight. Does he think I killed Stan?"

"Yes, I'm afraid he does, and so do many others. They all know that there was bad feelings between you and Stan, that you quarreled, that you had the opportunity —"

"Do you think I killed Stan?"

"No. I'm sure you didn't. But what can I say against so many?"

"But what reason in this world could make me want to kill my best friend?"

"He wasn't your best friend for a long time." Mac said.

"Yes. I was stupid to quarrel with him over —"

Then he dropped the bombshell.

"There are a few things I found here that I don't understand. It will only take me a short time to wind this up — I hope."

"Things you don't understand?"

"Yes — some papers and letters."

Here it is, Mac thought, without batting an eye. This is what I was afraid of.

# CHAPTER SIXTEEN

THE STORES ALONG the main street had not opened their doors yet for business. It was only eight-thirty. Miss Mc-Cormick paid for her breakfast at Kell's and headed toward the office. She was early, but it was such a beautiful morning, she wanted to take her time. She saw the flashy convertible streak past her toward the end of Ludington Street. There goes MacAllister, she thought. Driving as usual, like a maniac.

I wonder what she is doing up so early. This thought crossed Miss McCormick's mind as she sauntered leisurely along. It was nice to be able to walk to work. These days would soon be over and ice and snow would make walking a miserable task to be done — four times a day.

As she approached the entrance to the office building where the Norton Law Office was housed, she glanced down the side street. Mac's car was parked in the first parking space but Mac was nowhere in sight.

As she approached the office door she could see that it was open. For a moment she was startled, then she shrugged. Mac must have keys for the place, she told herself, why should I get all upset about this.

MacAllister was in the outer office, rifling through papers in the incoming mail file, her face a mask of fury.

To Mary McCormick this meant trouble. She didn't know what kind of trouble, but trouble nevertheless.

"I'm sorry, Mrs. Norton, I would have been here earlier if I'd have known you wanted to get in." Mary crossed to her desk, pulled out a drawer and tucked her purse inside.

"I'm sure you would have, Miss McCormick." Mac's voice was low-pitched. "And now let's quit playing around and get me the letter."

"Letter?" The young stenographer looked at the woman before her and wondered what she was talking about. "What letter?"

"There was to be a letter here for me yesterday. I want it."

"Mrs. Norton I know nothing about any letter. There was nothing in the mail yesterday for you."

"I know there was. I want it." Mac's voice was deadly calm.

"I'm sorry." Mary McCormick sat down at her desk and shrugged her shoulders. "Mr. Harris took care of the mail when it came in, I didn't see any of it. If you want the letter you'd better see him." She turned her back on Mac then, indifferent to the glares she was getting. I wonder why she's so excited about a letter, she thought, must be something in it she doesn't want anyone to see. I wonder if Rock got it and kept it?

But, it was obvious that Mac didn't believe the young

woman. She turned on her heel and stalked into the inner office and closed the door.

A moment later, Mary McCormick heard her talking. It was a one-sided conversation and, after a glance at the phone on her desk, Mary knew that Mac had called someone. The signal light was on. She could hear Mac's voice raised in annoyance and could hear sharp, short sentences but couldn't hear what was being said. She knew Mac was disturbed by not finding the letter. Evidently Rock had taken the letter, if it had come yesterday, and had not mentioned it to her. It must be *some* letter to have Mac going off like that.

She heard the sharp crash of the receiver slammed into its cradle and then Mac came storming out of the office.

"Tell Rock to call me when he comes in," she said.

"Yes, Mrs. Norton."

"The minute he comes in."

"Yes. I'll have him call."

She had turned back to her typewriter and was about to put paper in the machine when she felt the chill at the back of her neck. She turned around abruptly and surprised a glare on Mac's face. It was the face of a witch, a woman with a curse on her soul, a face both beautiful and damned. She was hypnotized by the eyes as they stared at her between half closed lids. She shivered. It was like walking across a grave at midnight, she thought. She could feel death around her.

Suddenly Mac realized that she was glaring and pulled herself back from the pit's edge. She shut her eyes and Mary watched the transformation. If anyone had told her that she would see this happen, she would have told them they were crazy. Her hands held the paper over the platform, she had no thought of moving. Nothing reached her brain except fear.

Mac laughed. It had an eerie sound, coming from within the body of a witch. It startled and brought Mary out of her trancelike state and she closed her eyes for a moment in disbelief and lowered her arms. She hated to open them. She knew Mac was watching her intently. She could feel the tenseness burn into her very brain. Then she forced them open. And Mac turned away.

No words passed between them as Mac left the office. Mary didn't trust herself to speak. She could have screamed but mere words were not there. So she said nothing. She watched Mac walk down the hall to the elevator. It was like watching the stalking of a panther.

Only when Mac disappeared from view could Mary let down. Then tears gushed forth in a torrent. Girls from offices on the floor heard her and came running. She couldn't explain. Deep, shattering sobs wracked her body until she cried herself out.

After assuring the girls she was all right, they left her alone. And it was then that she began to wonder why any letter coming in could create such a change in a person.

She closed and locked the outer door and went into the inner office. If she were going to snoop, she was not going to get caught at it.

Where would Rock put a letter he didn't want anyone to see. Mary had worked for Stanley Norton for a long time now and had never had occasion to wonder at anything he did. He had a special file that he kept locked.

She pulled open the top drawer and looked in each compartment. Nothing. Except a small cloth sack that held extra bolts for the desk. She had one in her desk, too. Without knowing why, she pulled open the drawstring of the little bag. There, with the bolts, was a small key. In a place where no one would ever look for it. The obvious place to hide it.

She took the key from the sack and unlocked the special file. She had no idea what she was looking for. And what she found was stunning and for a moment she closed her eyes. Then she began to read. The names on the top of each separate folder were names of most all the prominent people in town. People with money.

There was a tape in each folder and a typed transcript. She pulled one at random from the file. This was something which Stanley had carefully hidden from her. She had never seen either the tapes or the transcripts. What writing there seemed to be was not in Stanley's handwriting. She'd seen enough of Mac's writing to recognize it as hers.

It took only one paragraph to tell her what these folders contained. If they were all like this one, each folder had enough dynamite to blow up every household on the Drive. There were several folders with special delivery letters in them. This must be what Mac had been looking for. What Stanley had kept locked away from her, and what Rock had finally found. There was also a bank book. A bank book with MacAllister's name on it. Mary opened it. The last entry made was dated the same day Stanley Norton died.

She closed the file, locked it, and returned the key to the sack. Now she was sorry. Now she knew why Mac had been looking at her. Mac thought she knew about the special file. And now she did know. She knew and she didn't want to. And now Mary McCormick knew that Stanley Norton's death had not been natural. She shuddered. The chill of death was around her. And she was frightened.

She was sitting at her desk stirring the papers on top of it when Rock walked in.

He looked tired, she thought. If he had opened the file, he must know all the horrible truth. He must know that he held the death sentence of his former fiancee' in his hands.

"Hello there," he smiled with only his mouth.

"Hello."

"Are you ill,"

"No." Mary looked directly into his face then. "Mrs. Norton was here a few minutes ago looking for a letter."

"A letter." It was not a question. It was a statement.

"Yes." She was here when I came in."

Rock stopped then, as he was about to go into the inner office, and turned back. "Was she in that office?" he nodded toward the closed door.

"Yes. The door was open. She had been in there because I always leave it closed when I go. She was going through things on my desk when I came in."

"Did she say anything?" he asked.

Mary shuddered again as she remembered the fury and menace on the face of MacAllister. She shook her head.

Rock could see there had been some sort of mental tussle and said, "Why don't you get some fresh air, Mary? "There's nothing so important that it can't wait. You look terrible."

"Thanks, Rock—I think I will. I'm a little jittery I guess—" she wanted to say more.

Rock started to ask a question then stopped. Mary wondered what he was going to say. Had he received the letter in yesterday's mail—the one Mac was looking for? Had he found the file? Mary wanted to ask him but couldn't quite bring herself to speak.

"Did you bring your car today?" he asked.

"No—I walked. It was such a lovely day."

140

"Why don't you just take your car and go for a drive. You've been under quite a strain here the last few weeks. It'll do you good."

"It's in the garage—being fixed."

He didn't hesitate. "Take Stan's car. I used it this morning. I can pick it up later."

"Are you sure—?" Mary hesitated.

"Of course I'm sure! Go ahead. Go for a ride. You need some sunshine. When you come back you'll feel better."

Mary smiled at him. "I could stand some fresh air."

Rock handed her the keys. "I think I know why."

Her smile vanished. He was so true. Even fresh air could not erase the horrible truths from her mind. Rock hand sensed her need. Rock was that sort of person.

She glanced at the clock. Ten after ten. A short ride along the drive, near the shore would make her feel better. She loved driving.

Stan's last-year's-model car sat at the curb. She was grateful for the brief respite. Perhaps she could straighten things out in her mind. She relaxed behind the wheel and pulled away from the curb. The car drove smoothly as she headed down Ludington Street toward the Shore Drive.

She tried to sort out, in her mind, the sequence of events of the morning, but all she could see was the look of hate on Mac's face. She drove automatically. What had Mac found in the office? Why didn't she have a key to the file? Had Rock possession of the only key? And was Mac aware of the existence of the file? She must be. Her bank book was in it. Maybe she had been looking for the key, thinknig that Mary had it.

Traffic along the shore was non-existent and she was suddenly aware that she had passed the residential district and was out on the stretch south of town. There was a cut over she could take that circled around through the

141

countryside farmlands and when she reached it, she made the right hand turn. This would take her to U.S. 41 and back to town.

It was a gravel road, hilly and bumpy. After she had made the turn she wished she'd turned around and gone back on the highway. But it was too late now. She recognized several picnic spots along the way, then looked forward to the place where she had picnicked with her family, many times.

It was on the river, down a steep cut. The bridge across the swift moving water was at the bottom of the cut, just before the picnic area. She could catch glimpses of the river through the trees now. She would stop a moment, she decided. She hadn't driven out this way since the last family picnic last summer.

At the crest of the cut she took her foot from the accelerator and touched the brake. The downgrade was steep. Nothing happened. The car continued its speed over the crest and nosed downward with a sickening lurch. She slammed the brake pedal down to the floor and fright stiffened her grip on the wheel. As she tried to steer the jouncing car around deep holes in the road, the left front wheel hit a deep rut and wrenched the steering wheel from her hands. She was thrown sideways along the seat and the car careened downwards . . .

They found her body late that afternoon. Crushed between the wheel and the seat. The car was a mass of tangled wreckage.

The following inquiry disclosed a curious and unexplainable fact. One of the two brake linings was missing from the left front wheel.

# CHAPTER SEVENTEEN

KARI STIRRED RESTLESSLY, pounded her pillows into a fat bunch and leaned back. She was trying to relax as the doctor had prescribed. The dunking in the yacht harbor had not hurt her except for a slight case of the sniffles from the cold water. The reaction had set in after she had been put to bed. Her nerves had rebelled and she had collapsed more from the fright of an unknown stalker than from her dunking. She had no scratches or bruises, nothing the doctor could treat outwardly.

She slid out of bed and ran to the window. She could see the yacht harbor. She could look down the beach and almost pick out the route she had taken that night of the accident. She shivered and turned back to the bed and smoothed the covers. She couldn't stay there any longer, she thought. She had to get up, she had to see Rock.

Now that she had made up her mind to get up and stay up, she dressed hurriedly. A turquoise wool sweater over her white sheath brought out the flecks of color in her eyes. A quick swish of the brush through her blonde hair and a touch of color on her lips and she felt human again.

That is, she felt human for several minutes until she remembered that she was alone in this big house. Rock had hurried out just before lunch, saying that he had some more information to check at the office, and Bengy had taken Paul to the movie. Mac, after storming through the house ranting about the mess everything was in at the office, slammed out of the house and Kari had heard the screech out of the driveway, peeling rubber.

Wesley Bjornquist had not appeared yet. He had acquired the habit of dropping in at any hour of the day, for one reason or another, and usually stayed around until he'd managed to chat nonchalantly with each member of the household before he left.

Kari knew he was hoping one of the members would inadvertently drop some clue. He always ended up by asking her each time, if she couldn't remember anything which might aid him in finding out who had killed Stan. He sometimes acted as if he didn't believe that she'd been pushed in. But no matter how many questions he asked or how long he stayed, he always ended up with questions about Stanley Norton. About his murder.

Why did she think of it as murder? She asked herself this question now. It had never been mentioned that way. Why had it come out of her thoughts as murder? Had she been queried so much, heard so many answers, that now she, as well as Wesley Bjornquist, no longer thought of it as his death, but as his murder? She knew that Wesley was picking up bits of information here, pieces of information there, and weaving them into a noose for Rock. Of this she was sure.

When she mentioned the fact to Rock, he laughed at

her and scoffed at her fears. He didn't realize that slowly, Bjornquist was building up a case against him. Aided, of course, by bits and pieces from MacAllister. Little things, dropped in, but Kari knew they were planned, deliberately.

Rock, in his calm and collected way, would do nothing to protect himself, Kari mused. He, could not see how anyone would believe him guilty of the murder of his best friend. He would wait until it was too late to protest.

Wesley Bjornquist would build his case well. He would not make a move until he had all the facts — facts that would convict Rock. Facts that Mac and Bengy, at her command, had carefully suggested.

Now would be a good time to go over all the happenings, as much as she could remember, of what happened the night Stan had been killed. There would be no one coming in now to disrupt her actions. Everyone was gone. She was alone in the house.

Mentally she retraced her steps. She walked again — in thought, down the walk toward this big house on Lake Shore Drive. She remembered she approached and wondered where Rock was. She remembered how he had called to her from the darkness and how she had taken his arm and they had walked up the sidewalk to the huge pillared house in the dark.

She remembered her first impression of the old mansion. It had given her chills somehow. She remembered again, how she had shivered at the eerie picture it made in her mind. She remembered looking for Rock. She had not seen him until she got closer and he had called her.

Then she remembered something which she had not recalled until now. She remembered hearing the sound

of a slamming door, or it could have been a window. She
had not paid any attention to it at the time, but now
she remembered it. Now, knowing all the details that the
police had, she came to the inevitable conclusion. Only
Stanley was known to have been in the house, and since
it wasn't Stanley who had made that noise, then it must
have been someone else and that someone else could
only be Paul.

Kari left her room now and walked quietly down the
hall to Paul's room. Everything was in order. She wanted
to try the window, see if it made any noise that might
seem familiar to her, the noise that she'd heard the night
of the murder. She opened the window then. It actually
had no distinctive sound. It could sound like most any
window being raised and it wouldn't take much effort.
That's when she saw the small cupola just outside the
window. She leaned out to see where the opening
was. There was none on the outside. There must be some
other way.

She pulled her head in the window and closed it. That
was only part of the sound she'd heard. She opened and
closed the window several times to make sure that she
couldn't be mistaken. But there had been more to it than
that sound. There had been something else. It had a rusty,
squeaky sound, like something on an old hinge. She looked
around inside the room. Then she saw the small latched
door flush with the wall. It was concealed in the decorative paneling of the room and only on close inspection
would it ever be noticed.

She bent down to examine it. She ran her fingers lightly
around the decorative wood, until she came to the concealed button. She pressed it lightly, and, startled at the
result, stepped back. It was the rest of the sound she had
heard, rusty hinges and a thud as it closed.

146

And it was in Paul's room. Paul had been the only other person in the house the night of Stan's death. Paul must have been the one who had closed this window, its opening was in his room, his door had been locked. What had he seen from the cupola? She pressed the button again and the the hinged door flipped open. By crouching down she could enter the tiny cubicle.

The interior was nothing more than a shell bottom half wood, top half windows, except that a round cushioned seat was built so that one could sit and look outside, over rooftops and through the trees, and have an unobstructed view of the surrounding area. Today, the view was beautiful. Kari sat on the bench and looked out, wondering just what Paul had seen the night his father had died. She turned and looked out toward the back of the house. She had a practically unobstructed view of the grounds. But that isn't what surprised her most. From this spot one had a balcony seat view of the library. The windows, where they jutted out in an L-shaped bay were in a direct line of vision with the floor below. Kari could see Stan's desk and chair, and she could see part way across the room. If anyone had been in the room, near the desk, Kari could have seen them. She could have seen Stan if he had been sitting at his desk.

She realized then, that there had been a witness to the happenings in the library, whatever they were. Had Paul been in the cupola? Had he been an eye witness to the murder of his father? Is that why the child had been so terrified, terrified of everyone and everything?

She squeezed back out into Paul's room and closed the small door. It closed tightly with a dull thud. Yes, that was the rest of the sound she had heard the night she and Rock stood there in the darkness trying to find a way into the house.

147

It wasn't until then that she realized there was someone in the room with her. She could hear heavy breathing. She was almost afraid to turn around. Whoever it was had made no sound when it came in. It was standing just around the other side of the huge canopied bedstead, just out of sight.

There was no place to retreat. Was it the killer? Was it waiting for her to step farther into the room so that it could grab her? The hair on the nape of her neck stood out and a chill held her immobile for a moment. Then she took a step forward. There was no use trying to hide.

She took the step. Paul's frightened face peered up at her around the corner of the bed. His eyes were wide open, frightened. She collapsed on the bed.

"Paul!" she said, "You scared me half to death.

' I didn't know who it was. I could hear someone in the peek-a-boo when I came in but I didn't know it was you." He came around to Kari's side.

"The peek-a-boo?"

He pointed to the cupola.

She was about to ask him a question.

"Don't ask," he cried. "Please don't ask me anything! I —" then he started to cry. Huge, gulping sobs shook his small, tense body and he threw himself into her arms. He was shaking as she held him close.

Kari's thoughts raced. Poor child. He's seen so much that he can't forget it. It's with him every minute. Of what he had seen — frightened half to death. It was in his eyes every time he looked at his mother.

She brushed the hair away from his damp forehead. "There, there, don't cry, Paul. Everything will be all right, don't worry now."

Paul's arms tightened around her neck and his sobbing

stopped momentarily. "No. Don't ask, Kari. Please don't ask anyone!"

"But, Paul, —" she protested.

"I don't want you —" he gulped, "Just don't ask."

Another warning, this time from Paul. This was the third warning. First, Stan had suggested she leave. Then Bengy. Now Paul had added his warning in another form.

The sobs had subsided now and he went to the windows and gazed out across the bay. He completely ignored her now as she walked from his room.

At the top of the stairs she could hear Mac's voice. She couldn't understand any of the words but she could tell by the inflections that they were vicious as only Mac-Allister's words could be. She could hear no other voice, then, the door partly opened and Bengy Florrietto quickly slid through and ducked. A book came sailing out and just missed his head. For a brief instant, Kari could see Mac glaring through the opening. The door banged shut.

Throwing things must be part of the MacAllister technique, Kari thought to herself as she continued down the stairs. Perhaps the white spot on the hall carpet had occured the same way. As a result of Mac's temper. Now Kari could see explanations for several of the things she had wondered about. Mac had thrown something — at someone. She had been angry enough to throw something at someone. Pieces of the puzzle were beginning to fit, to drop comfortably into place.

Stanley evidently had been the target on the tragic night. There had been no trace on his clothes, so obviously, if Mac had thrown anything at him, she had not hit him with it. But could the quarrel have started the whole tragedy? Could he have argued with her over something — possibly the letters, the blackmail scheme, or

149

over using his office downtown as a nest for her intrigue?

Could there have been a quarrel — enough of a quarrel to start a heart attack? Stan could have made the library and his desk. But where had Mac disappeared to? She and Bengy had been at the house. Paul must have heard the commotion, probably even saw the fight, if there had been one. Did Mac know that Paul had been a witness to whatever had gone on that evening? Was that the reason that Paul cringed every time he saw his moher?

At the inquest Mac had denied being at the house at the time of Stanley's heart attack. She and Bengy were at the dinner. Stanley, too, was supposed to have attended. Why hadn't he gone with his wife and Bengy? And, if he'd had a heart attack when Mac was there, why hadn't she given him his nitro? But she had been at the dinner. She had plenty of witnesses to that fact. But if this was true, if MacAllister had nothing to do with Stan's heart attack, why was Paul so frightened? At the trial she had said nothing about a quarrel with her husband. Why hadn't she mentioned it?

Kari left the house and walked around the grounds. She looked up from the driveway and took special notice of the cupola. It was fairly well concealed by the architecture of the house. It blended with the exterior until, unless one was particularly looking for it.

Paul being the kind of child he was, evidently spent many hours gazing from the circular room. When he wanted to hide, it was a good place to go. Anyone going into his room would never think of looking there for him.

He must have been there the night of his father's heart attack. Perhaps he had seen it happen? Why, then, when he saw his father undoubtedly in agony, had he not raced down to help him, or to call help?

Somehow she was missing something. So obvious perhaps that normally it would never be noticed at all. What was it? She turned back to the house asking herself these questions. What was it she was overlooking, so obvious that it was taken for granted. It was only a faint memory of something, but evidently something she had taken for granted. She searched for it in her mind, almost found it, then lost it again.

She closed her eyes, it was there in her mind, of that she was sure. Why was it eluding her? Then the picture of an empty cocktail shaker sprang to the screen of her mind and she opened her eyes wide.

That was it! Wesley kept insisting that she must have seen something that seemed out of place, or a bit unusual. Just any little thing that she could remember. But, until now, the cocktail shaker had not entered her mind. She remembered, too, that Rock had commented on it being there and that he had tasted the few drops left in the bottom. But, because he'd said Stanley didn't drink, she took for granted that there perhaps had been dinner cocktails and that the shaker hadn't been cleaned or put away.

She hurried toward the kitchen. Signe, the all-purpose day maid was just finishing the dishes.

"Good morning, Signe," Kari said. "I wonder if you have a cocktail shaker?"

"Ya," Signe dried her hands on one corner of her apron, "Up there in the cupboard." She pointed to the top shelf. "I cannot reach it, without a stool."

Kari, standing on tip-toe could just reach it and in a moment it was in her hands. She opened the top, pulling the glass shaker top apart. Had it been washed before it had been put away? It was the same one she'd seen on the desk when they'd found Stan. Oddly enough, there seemed to be a film in the bottom of the shaker. Whoever had grabbed it had picked it up hurriedly and shoved it back on the shelf without washing or rinsing it out. She replaced the top and carried it out of the kitchen with her.

She wondered, briefly, why the police had not noticed the shaker on the desk. Perhaps because it was empty and there had been no glasses around, they had taken for granted that it was a decorative piece. Could there be any connection between this and Stan's death? Kari was part way up the front stairway when she heard a key in the lock.

With the shaker in her hand, and no convenient place to hide it, she hoped it was Rock. He had said he'd be back soon.

It was Rock. He opened the door, stepped in and leaned back against it and closed his eyes. His face was drawn and tensely white. He looked as if he'd seen a ghost.

Kari dropped the shaker on the stairs, pushed it in the corner near the wall and ran down the stairs. His arms went out to hold her close, tight against him. She could feel the throbbing bump of his heart and then his lips were pressed to her forehead, to her eyes, then to her lips.

"Rock — darling — what has happened?"

Rock stepped away from the door then and shook his head as if to clear away a bad dream. His lips against her hair, he said, "Kari, you've got to leave this place, right now — today. You can go to my place in Milwaukee.

"I won't leave you, Rock."

His hands cradled her face as he looked into her eyes. "Darling, you must go. If anything happened to you," his voice broke, "I don't know what I'd do." His lips against hers, he said, "You've got to! Now!"

"No, Rock."

"You have to."

"No."

"Why must I?"

Rock could hardly get the next words out of his mouth. "Mary McCormick is dead!"

"Mary McCormick? Stanley's secretary?"

Rock nodded his head.

"Oh, Rock — no —" Kari looked tensely into his face, "What happened?"

Briefly, as they walked toward the library, he explained how he'd told Mary to take the car and go for some fresh air after her encounter with MacAllister.

"You were supposed to be in that car, Rock!"

'I know that. That's what makes me sick. Why Mary? Why should she have to die?"

Neither of them heard the key in the front door lock. Neither of them saw the door open. MacAllister stood there, with the sun behind her, looking at them. With flaming hair, bewiched by the sun, she looked like an angel in pale lavender. Only her face had no resemblance to an angel. First, her blue eyes held surprise, then sparkled dangerously and, after the first shock of seeing Rock and Kari standing there in each other's arms, hate.

Kari read all this in one glance. She hates to see Rock with me. She wants Rock to herself. But why did she look as if she'd seen a ghost?

Rock kept his arms around Kari. His eyes were leveled on MacAllister, almost as if he were seeing her face for the first time.

"I'm still here, Mac." he said evenly.

MacAllister closed her eyes to a tense slit. "I'm a little surprised."

"I knew you would be."

"Oh. You knew?"

"Yes. Finally. And I know the answers now, Mac." Rock spoke these words quietly.

MacAllister came inside and shut the door. She walked past them, into the library and closed the door quietly. She must remember to be calm, quiet. Not let Rock see that his words had made any impression. Why had he said what he did? There was nothing he could do. He couldn't prove anything. He merely thought he could. He could suspect. But, without any proof, what else could he do?

Once inside the library her anger exploded. She didn't dare make any noise but she paced, like a caged tigress, back and forth, mouthing foul words under her breath. She wanted to scream them out loud, to throw things, to hurt! How had this failed? She planned so carefully, every tiny detail, yet there he stood. What had gone wrong? Hadn't things gone according to schedule? She knew he always took the long road down the shore to the cliff side cut-out on his way to the office. She had counted on this. He'd always driven there when problems worried him. He always said he could think better down there, looking over the water. He'd said it soothed his nerves, made him think straight.

The cut-out was actually only a short distance from the highway. It was an unloading pier years before, during logging days when small boats hauled logs. The pier had fallen into decay until only the cliff itself remained, jutting out over the rocks and water, thirty feet below.

But Rock was here. Why hadn't he taken that drive this morning? Where was the car? It had not been parked in its usual place when she drove up to the house. He said he knew the answers now. Had he found the files that Stanley had locked away so carefully from her? It he had found those letters and the blackmail evidence as she suspected, then he could be her executioner.

MacAllister continued pacing. What had happened? She had carefully planned to eliminate him, even though he still made her blood run hot in her veins. The telephone broke her train of thoughts and she lifted the receiver.

"Yes?"

"Mrs. Norton?" It was was Wesley Bjornquist.

"This is Mrs. Norton."

'There has been an accident. Mr. Norton's car."

"An accident —?" Mac hesitated, Rock had not mentioned that he'd had an accident. Was that what he meant when he said he had all the answers? "What do you mean?" her voice was even, she must not display anything more than the usual concern for a damaged vehicle.

"I mean that there has been an accident. Your husband's car is completely demolished."

Why didn't Rock tell me he'd had an accident, Mac thought. "I hope no one was hurt," she said.

"I'll be right over. Please see that everyone remains there." Bjornquist's voice was expressionless.

MacAllister hung up the receiver. Rock had somehow escaped the accident. Now what? She knew that he was her sworn enemy now. Nothing she could do, could change that. It hadn't been easy, like getting rid of Stanley had been. That had been a breeze. And there was no evidence against her. She and Bengy had been at the dinner . . . When she finished with this town, the stigma of being from the other side of the tracks would be completely erased.

Wesley Bjornquist would believe her story against Rock. Now that he was still alive she must play her hand with care. She must play it just right. Bjornquist was already sure that Rock did it. All she had to do would be to offer a few suggestions here, a few there.

When she heard the front doorbell ring, she stopped pacing and opened the library door just in time to see Rock ushering in Wesley Bjornquist and Bengy. She wondered why Wesley had picked Bengy up. Bengy looked nervous . For a moment his eyes met her's.

They all moved down the hall toward the library. Mac stood waiting for them, framed there in the door.

Wesley Bjornquist pointed to the easy chairs and said, "Might as well sit down."

Rock and Kari sat together on the leather chaise. Bengy went toward MacAllister and pulled an occasional chair closer to where she sat. His hands fumbled with and lit a cigarette. He took long drags on it, blowing the smoke out in short puffs. He glanced at Mac, out of the corner of his eyes, trying to drain some of her self-confidence for himself. She could sense his fear.

Then Wesley spoke. "There has been an accident." No one moved. "An accident of murder!"

MacAllister started inwardly. What was this crazy fool talking about? Rock was right here in the room. Couldn't he see that for himself? Was he trying to trap someone — her for instance? She laughed a short, quick laugh. "But we're all here," she said.

"No. We're not all here, Mrs. Norton. Mary McCormick is dead."

"Mary McCormick?" Mac got the two words out finally.

156

Bengy, startled and unable to contain himself, jittered around on his chair. His eyes were on Mac's face to see what she was going to do.

She looked at Rock. He was looking directly at her, waiting for her reply.

"What happened? This is terrible." She hesitated briefly, "I don't know why this concerns us, Mr. Bjornquist."

"Miss McCormick was driving your late husband's car, Mrs. Norton."

Mac's eyes flicked to Rock's and then back to the sheriff. "I don't know how she happened to be using his car in the first place, and I'm sure I was nowhere around. I'm sorry, but what else can I do. I'm not responsible for Miss McCormick!" She made her voice sound indignant to cover up the cold dread that was beginning to seep through.

"The car had been tampered with, Mrs. Norton. By someone who had a motive and the opportunity." He paused and looked around the small group. "And we'll find out who did it."

"I'm sure you will," Mac said.

He turned to Rock. "Where were you this morning?"

"I was at the office, working."

"Was Miss McCormick there?"

"Yes. She was there when I came in."

"Was she in the habit of taking a drive during working hours?"

"No. Not that I'm aware of."

"Then how do you account for the fact that she had Mr. Norton's car?"

Rock didn't answer immediately. He looked at Mac. "She was very upset when I arrived this morning."

"Upset? What over?"

"I'm not sure." Rock didn't want to mention Mac's

**157**

name now. Not until he found out more about what had happened.

"You must have some idea."

"Someone had been in the office before she got there. I guess they upset things on her desk."

"Had this ever happened before?"

"Not to my knowledge, no."

"Do you know who it was?"

Before Rock could answer Mac interrupted. "I'm sure this has very little to do with the accident. I was in the office earlier. I see no reason why Miss McCormick should be upset. After all, I believe I do have a right to go in the office of my own business, do I not?"

"I see no reason why not." The sheriff turned back to Rock. "But that doesn't explain why Miss McCormick had Mr. Norton's car. Did you know she was taking it?"

"Yes. In fact I told her to go out for some air. Since her own car was in the garage I told her to take Stan's. If the car was tampered with then that means someone expected me to be the driver, not Miss McCormick."

"But why should anyone want to harm you?" Wesley Bjornquist said.

"I have no idea. Unless I'm getting too close to some of the truths about Mr. Norton's death." Rock said this softly and his eyes lifted to Mac's for just an instant.

"What do you mean?"

"Oh — nothing in particular. Just that some of the pieces are dropping into place."

"Well, if none of you can enlighten me any further I'll get back to the lab. They must have run some tests by now. Don't any of you leave town. There will be more questions later."

Bjornquist turned away from the little group and let himself out of the library. For a moment no one spoke.

158

Then Rock and Kari rose and started out the door.

Mac broke the silence then with, "Rock I'd like to see you alone."

Rock turned and looked back. "Alone?"

Kari pulled her hand from his, "I'll wait for you in the hall," she pulled the door shut behind her. She headed for the stairway where she'd dropped the cocktail shaker when Rock had come in. It was still there, in the corner of the stairway where she'd pushed it.

Without quite understanding why she was doing this, and without any particular reason, she turned back toward the library, the shaker under her arm.

She almost bumped into Rock. He was just coming out of the door. Kari walked in past him and thought he'd turned to follow her. Actually he wanted to get out of the room.

Bengy and MacAllister were standing near the desk, Stan's desk. Her face was a mask of fury.

It wasn't until Kari was close to her that Mac saw the cocktail shaker tucked carefully under her arm. It was the cocktail shaker she'd hurriedly pushed away on the top shelf after the police had left the night of Stan's heart attack. It had attracted no attention because of the fact that she'd washed and put away the glasses. She'd forgotten the shaker in her haste to leave for the banquet, to get out of there before anyone arrived. Later, there had been no time to wash it, no opportunity.

Bengy saw the shaker at the same instant. His face lost its color. His eyes focused on the shaker as if it were a crystal ball. It was the first time he'd seen it since the night he'd tried to revive Stan with it's contents.

His words startled everyone. They came out more as a nervous reaction than from any other reason. "At least you didn't kill her the same way, Mac."

# CHAPTER EIGHTEEN

MACALLISTER WAS standing close to Bengy. She lashed out with her hand and her tongue at the same time. The loud crack of flesh on flesh as her hand struck him across the side of the face startled Kari. "You crazy fool! Shut up!"

But it was too late. Kari looked at them both, almost overcome with the horrible truth. "Yes, I suspected something like this but I couldn't actually believe it. I can't see how you could do a thing like that. It had to be you. You killed your own husband. You killed him!" She turned to speak to Rock, thinking he was behind her. "Rock —" she said, then gasped.

MacAllister laughed. "Your precious Rock left as you came in, my dear. So if you think you can use any of this against me, please think long before you start anything. It would be your word against mine. Of course I should say mine and Bengy's."

MacAllister put her hand on Bengy's shoulder. He was

calmer now. But in the place of fear, his face reflected another strong emotion. His temper had exploded and his face was red with anger. He was angry because he'd spoken his thoughts aloud, had, without thinking, exposed the horrible secret that had been haunting him night and day for the past two weeks.

"I don't think Bengy would lie about it," Kari said.

"I don't think Bengy has much choice," Mac said, "that's if he wants to save his own skin."

Bengy seemed to straighten up a little as MacAllister spoke. He shook his head dazed at the turn of events and walked over to Kari. He stood over her looking down and suddenly was frightened of this man who had the spell of MacAllister Norton woven around his heart.

Then he spoke, slowly, as if in a stupor. "I didn't hear a thing. They'd hang me for sure." He paused a moment. "I'd hate to hang for something I tried to prevent."

"Shut up, Bengy. Shut your mouth before you say another word." Mac spat out.

"Yeah, Mac. I'm just a coward. Just a coward —" his words dwindled off into nothingness as he turned and walked from the room.

Kari shuddered when she pulled her glance away from Bengy.

"It won't do you any good to tell that little fable," Mac goaded with persistancy. "No one would believe such a story — and anyway, they don't know you. They know me!"

"I don't care about the story. I heard you, I heard Bengy. You killed your husband." Kari's voice broke.

"Don't be melodramatic, my dear," Mac purred, " nothing can stop me. Nothing."

"I'll find some way to make you tell the truth," Kari fought back with words. "Somehow I'll make them believe me, even thought they don't know me. They knew Stan. Rock will believe me."

"I don't think Rock will do any such thing," Mac said. "In the first place he won't believe you, and in the second place he is the suspect, not me."

"But you will be. Believe me, you will be."

"They'll laugh you right out of town."

"I don't think so, MacAllister. No — I don't think they will. Not when I've explained it to them."

Mac smiled. No one would believe the story of this girl, especially when Mac would deny it, laugh it off.

"I'll call Wesley Bjornuist for you if you want to tell him now," Mac needled. "Go ahead. I'd like to have you try it. After you get through with your little story I'll deny it and show you how wrong you are." She walked around now to stand in front of Kari. "They'll believe me."

"Rock won't believe you. He will know the truth." Kari said.

MacAllister hated to think of Rock. He had changed so much. He had been her slave such a short time ago. Now his eyes held nothing but contempt and pity for her. She could feel it every time they faced each other. Yes, he would believe Kari. When Kari told him this then he would know for sure that if Mac had killed Stanley — with Bengy's help — then she had also killed Mary McCormick. That would be simple to figure out. How she did it would be hard to prove. She had left no trace when she and Bengy had removed the brake lining. Her brothers had always fixed cars and she'd seen them take cars apart hundreds of times when she was young. It had been no trick at all to remove one drum. He would also know that the accident had been meant for him, not for Mary McCormick. He would know all this but he would have no proof. He would not be able to find any proof.

The most important thing now was how to keep Kari from telling Rock what she had heard. That Mac had admitted killing Stanley. Rock would believe anything Kari told him. How could she keep this snip of a girl from telling Rock? Only one thing would keep her quiet. That was Rock himself. She would do anything for him. She would do anything to help him and to prove that he had not killed Stanley. Why hadn't she thought of this before? Kari would not talk. Not if Rock's whole future were at stake.

Once again MacAllister knew she had the upper hand. Her face relaxed and she smiled lazily, a feline smile. Her blue eyes seemed to change in color as she closed her lids to slits. She began to pace again, sure that she had found the solution.

"All right, Kari," she said finally, "tell Rock. Call him in here and tell him right now. Let's get this straightened out. Tell Wesley too, if you think it will do any good. But —" the ominous note was again in her voice, "if you tell anyone, I shall tell them what you told me."

"What I told you?" Kari looked at Mac in surprise.

"Yes. What you told me."

"But I didn't tell you anything."

"Oh, but you did! You told me that Rock wouldn't give Stanley his nitro pills when he had that heart attack. That's what killed him, you know."

"This is ridiculous, Mac. I never told you any such thing." Kari protested.

"It's my word against yours. You told me —" Mac's eyes were dark, slate-colored slits surrounded by flaming red hair.

Kari seemed to wilt. "It would kill Rock's future to have anything like that happen. Mac — you would do this to Rock?"

"If I have to," Mac answered. "A lot of people would believe the story. They are feeling sorry for me now, they can be told anything and they'll believe it. Especially with a few tears thrown in." Mac's grin was wicked. "He'd be ruined. His career would be gone."

"Knowing this, you'd still do it?" Kari couldn't believe it yet.

"I'll save my own neck any way I know how. And I can be pretty convincing when I put myself out."

"Yes," Kari said.

MacAllister watched Kari and she knew, by the look on Kari's face that she would never tell any of what had transpired in this room. And certainly she wouldn't tell Rock. Kari would take no chances on ruining Rock's great future in dermatology. No, Kari would never tell now.

But MacAllister could not let it stand at that. She continued needling Kari. "It's too late to do anything, anyway. You can't do anything about Stanley. He's dead and buried." Her voice was harsh. "You know what happened, and still you can't use it — tell it to anyone. And you can't stay here. I'm sick of seeing you around! You'd better go. Forget Rock. If you don't —" her voice was threatening now and Kari shivered in spite of herself.

She looked straight into Mac's face now.

Mac's eyes faltered and shifted. She didn't like what she saw it Kari's eyes. But she knew that she was safe from Kari. She wouldn't tell Rock.

"That's one thing I won't do, Mac. I won't leave until Rock leaves."

"But Rock can't leave until the investigation is over. Bjornquist told Rock that last week. There are too many strings left untied — too many loose ends he said." She laughed mirthlessly.

"Rock won't leave until he knows the truth. If I don't tell him he'll find out in some other way." Kari raised her hand to stop Mac from interrupting. "Oh, don't worry. I won't say one word. Of that you can be sure."

"I am sure that you won't talk but I'm sick of seeing you around the house. I can't come into the house but what you're under my nose. I'd suggest you leave today. Now!"

"No. I intend to stay, MacAllister. I don't intend to leave until Rock leaves. When he is finished then we'll be very happy to go. And you can't make us leave. What would all your friends say? That you put us out? They'd be sure to think something was wrong. They'd talk.

"Have you no fear of what might happen?"

"Fear?" Kari asked. "Yes, I have fear but I also have faith. Faith, that this will all be taken care of. I love Rock."

MacAllister snorted in derision. "Love! What do you know about love!"

"I know that without it, there isn't much point in living. Without someone to think about, to do things for, to help when they're in trouble — what is there to life?" said Kari.

"I think about myself. That's what life is — dog eat dog! And I'm tired of being eaten!"

"You must be a very miserable and lonely person, Mac-Allister." Kari, for a brief moment, had pity in her heart for this woman, who was wasting her life.

"I'm not miserable," MacAllister said, "nor lonely." She smiled to herself. "I'll have money."

Kari knew it was no use talking to her. She shook her head.

"Just don't try anything funny," MacAllister said.

"Are you afraid?" Kari asked.

"Afraid?"

"Afraid that someone might talk? You were afraid you hadn't done your job good enough the night Stanley died. I watched your face. You were afraid, Mac. You were afraid he wouldn't die! You were afraid of what he might do if he recovered. It will always be like that, Mac."

MacAllister had no answer. She was angry. Her face was the color of a death mask. She would have to get rid of this girl who had taken Rock away and who now threatened her with exposure.

"Don't even think it, Mac. I'll leave a sealed letter — to be opened if I die." Kari stood her ground.

MacAllister's fury mounted but she said nothing.

"You'd hate to have your schemes made public, Mac. All the things you've built up. You'd be back on the North Shore again! Think it over." Kari turned on her heel and walked out of the library.

# CHAPTER NINETEEN

Kari hurried. She must find Rock. Where had he gone? She heard his voice coming from the hallway. "Rock —?"

Rock put his finger to his lips as she came toward him. He was on the phone.

"Rock, I have to tell you something —"

"Not now."

"Yes!"

"Sh —!" He motioned her to silence, then said, "I'll be through here in a few minutes . . . wait . . ."

But Kari, terrified by the thought the perhaps she would not have time to do what she knew she must do, bolted and fled past him up the stairs and into her room.

Rock, a bit startled, resumed his conversation. Wesley Bjornquist was on the other end of the line. Then, he was aware that someone else had come up behind him. Rock turned abruptly and faced Bengy, who tried to act casual.

"Just a minute," Rock said into the phone, "did you want something, Bengy?" he asked.

"Only waiting to use the phone," Bengy answered. "No hurry though." He fidgeted a little and couldn't face Rock's direct gaze.

"I'll be a few minutes, and this is a private conversation," he said.

"Oh, sorry. I'll be out on the porch. Let me know when you get through?"

Rock nodded, and waited for Bengy to get out of range of his next words. "What did you find?"

Bjornquist's voice was sharp as he answered. "Someone tampered with the brake lining all right. One lining was missing and the other had been tampered with. What little braking power there was, would only be good if you were driving on level ground. She must have applied to brake on the down grade and there just was nothing there."

"It was meant for me," Rock said.

"How do you figure?"

"I had the car. I've had it to use ever since I've been taking care of Stan's estate. Whoever did this was aiming at me."

"Or Mary McCormick was close —" Wesley interrupted.

"No. I think they were after me. Mary certainly hadn't anything to do with any of this. What do you mean by — she could have been close?"

"She had every opportunity to know Stan's business. Have you been hiding something — something that Mary McCormick might have just realized she knew — something that might pertain to Stan's death?"

Rock's face was stern as he answered. "I've told you over and over — whoever did this has built a beautiful frame — a frame that will be hard to crack. But, I did not kill Stan!"

"So you said," came back the quiet reply. "But what

168

could Mary have found out?" Bjornquist kept coming back to this question.

"I'm sure she didn't find out anything. I've been working in that office ever since —" he stopped abruptly and turned his head quickly, just in time to see Bengy pull sharply away from the screen door. Obviuosly he had been listening to the conversation.

Rock put down the receiver saying, "Just a minute —" and walked softly over to the door. He stood there for long enough to know that Bengy was standing close to the door on the other side, listening to every word that was said.

Satisfied that he had discovered Bengy, before he said anything he didn't want heard, Rock walked back and picked up the receiver again.

"Sorry Wesley, didn't mean to keep you waiting. Tell you what — I'll come down to see you. There's a few things I want to get straightened out."

"Good, I'll be waiting."

As Rock hung up the receiver, he could hear Bengy move stealthily away from the other side of the door and begin to whistle softly.

What was the sudden interest in his conversation? Why had Bengy been hovering over him today? Rock asked himself as he started back toward the library. As he approached, the door flung open violently.

Mac came out but when she saw Rock she stopped and waited. Her eyes snapped with subdued fire as she waited for him. Bengy came in from the porch. Rock saw Mac's eyes flick quietly to Bengy and back. He could not tell whether there had been some sort of signal between them or not.

"Where's Kari?" Mac asked.

Rock was about to answer, when Bengy broke in, "She isn't here."

He'd been listening so close — he certainly must have heard her. Rock closed his eyes for a split second.

Mac's face was a sneer and her glare turned from Rock to Bengy, but Bengy was paying no attention to her. He turned around went back ont on the porch and stood puffing on a cigarette.

MacAllister watched him leave. She made no comment. Rock could sense that she was preoccupied. She walked past him toward the stairs. He knew Kari had gone up, he remembered now that he'd heard the slam of her bedroom door. He saw MacAllister hesitate slightly as she stepped over the faint white spot on the hallway carpet. She was halfway up the stairs when the front doorbell rang simultaniously with the opening of the door, and Wesley Bjornquist hurried in, out of breath.

"Mary McCormick was murdered! The lab just got through checking and found a half a dozen positive clues."

Rock watched MacAllister's face. He said nothing, just watched her. After the first start of surprise at the word murder, her face became composed, Rock thought — and I thought I knew this woman.

"What happened? You said it was murder?" Mac said calmly.

"Yes. But the murderer made a mistake."

Mac was impatient. "How did it happen?"

"Someone tampered with your husband's car, and it had no brakes. She went down the steep incline at the river, near the picnic grounds. Evidently, out of control. The steering wheel crushed her."

"But that isn't murder."

"It was a planned murder, Mrs. Norton. But planned

170

for someone else. He glanced at Rock, who stood listening and watching Mac's face.

"For whom?" Mac was insistent.

Rock said, coldly, "For me."

MacAllister started slightly when he broke in. She looked at him then, with the first touch of fear that she'd displayed. She dropped her eyes so that he couldn't see the fear and unrest that Bjornquist's words had caused.

"I'm sure you must be exaggerating all this. Why would anyone want to kill you?"

"There could be several reasons," Rock answered, looking straight into her eyes, "I am only trying now to figure out which one would be the most motivating. Right now, I'm not sure. But I will be soon." He looked upstairs toward Kari's room. "In fact, I shall know a great deal very soon."

MacAllister smiled then. She was sure that Kari wouldn't say anything to Rock. She would keep her silence. Right now, the job was to get Bjornquist off this latest trail.

"Wesley, as you know, I am very busy. Is there something you want of me or may I get back to my work?" Her tone was caustic.

"I want to know a few things. Just where is the car kept at night?" he asked.

"In the garage of course."

"Is the garage usually locked?"

"Yes. We've had several robberies in this neighborhood. Nothing serious. But we lock the garage to discourage any ideas." MacAllister drew a deep breath. Now was the time to drop a few hints. "Of course since Rock has been using the car, I don't pay any attention to where it is. Since he's had it continuously, I'm sure he is better qualified to answer these questions than I."

Bjornquist seemed to consider this. He turned to Rock. "Where was the car last night?"

"In it's usual place. I drove it in the garage and locked the door."

"So no one could get at it then — I mean, without you knowing it this morning?" Bjornquist asked.

"I suppose someone could have gotten in and done what they wanted to do. I wouldn't necessarly know about it until I started to drive, or until the accident happened to me."

MacAllister interjected a remark. "All these accidents seem to have happened since you came to town, Rock."

Rock exploded. "Damn it, Mac, you know I didn't kill Stan!" His face was white, then turned crimson with rage. "Suggesting these things to Wes here, turns a little of the heat off you, doesn't it?"

Bjornquist broke in, "I'm turning the heat off no one! And what she says doesn't alter things either. I'm still keeping the book open on your activities the night of the murder. Now this! What else can one think?"

MacAllister tried to conceal the delight she got from this sudden outburst. She had planted the seed of doubt in Bjornquist's mind, without being too obvious about it. He wouldn't admit it, probably didn't realize that Rock was still the prime suspect.

"I didn't mean to upset you, Rock. I'm sure that Welsey will not hold the things I say of too much consequence, will you Wes?" Her question was like a command to agree with her.

Rock wondered just what MacAllister had on the Chief of Police, that he had to cater to her. Or did he really think that he, Rock, had really been the killer. Up until this moment Rock had not given any thought to the fact that Wesley Bjornquist might consider him a good prospect for the crime.

"I'm not one to be answering questions, Mrs. Norton," he said, "I just ask them."

But MacAllister was not to be stopped so easily. "What did they find?"

Bjornquist looked at her quizzically. "You will know soon enough."

Rock looked at MacAllister, wondering how she would take this refusal to divulge information. She was taking it as he expected she would, with angry acceptance.

"If you're going back downtown, Wesley, I'd like to ride with you," Rock broke the silence with his request.

"Fine. I was going to ask you to anyway. I'd like to discuss a few things with you." Wesley started out the door and Rock followed, leaving MacAllister standing. On the porch he hesitated. Kari had wanted to talk to him about something.

"Can you wait just a minute till I see what Kari wanted?" he asked Bjornquist.

"I'm sorry. I have to get back immediately. They were setting up some other tests when I left, and said they'd be through shortly. We can't delay. Every minute gives the killer a chance to commit another crime."

Rock looked back over his shoulder as he followed Bjornquuist down the steps and out to the car. Kari would be safe in her room. He hoped she would stay there.

# CHAPTER TWENTY

MacALLISTER PACED BACK and forth across the library. Back and forth between the desk and the windows. She was so deep in vicious thought that she failed to hear Kari come downstairs and go out the front door. Mac-Allister was busy trying to drill information from Signe, the maid, that she didn't hear the front door close.

"You were here all day. You must have seen her! Where is she?" The words poured out like bullets from an automatic. Words like a whip lash, words the beat against Signe's ears.

"I do not know. I did not see her. I pay no attention to things which do not concern me."

"Don't lie to me!"

"I am not lying. I do not lie about things!"

To make Signe talk, MacAllister was forcing the issue. She did not realize that some people only disappear within their shell when questioned in this manner. Signe was used to these tantrums of MacAllister's. She'd stayed on only because of Stanley Norton.

"But you certainly must have seen whether she went out or not? Bengy said she was not here."

"I know nothing." Signe was adamant.

MacAllister stopped then. She stood close to her, tapping a nervous tatoo with her toe. "Look at me!" she ordered.

Signe raised her eyes and gazed calmly into MacAllister's face.

"Where did she go?"

"I have no idea."

"Did she call anyone? Did she see Rock before he left?"

"I do not know."

"Oh, damn you! I don't know — I don't know!" she mocked, "is that all you can say?"

But Signe didn't flinch. Instead, she said, "May I go now?"

"Yes! Go!" MacAllister turned abruptly and strode back to the window and stood with her back to Signe.

There had been no phone calls. Of this she was sure. But had Kari the time to write a letter, or any kind of message, and dispose of it since she'd last been seen? If she only knew what she was looking for.

She was glad that Rock had gone with Wesley Bjornquist. There wasn't much he could do, one way or the other. He was the prime suspect. Let Wesley Bjornquist spend his time trying to fit clues against Rock. She had dropped plenty of them for this purpose. It would keep him busy until she could get rid of Kari and her precious letter. Oh, he was good for most phases of his job, but in the matter of murder, he was easy to lead astray.

First, she must find the evidence that Kari said she would leave. It must be in the house.

175

There was just a chance that she might have written something and left it up where Rock would get it as soon as he came in. MacAllister hurried up the long stairway and Kari's room.

Evidently Kari had waited her chance and had gone out when no one was thinking. Strange Bengy hadn't seen her go. Mac bit her bottom lip and the thought crossed her mind that perhaps Bengy was getting too jittery to think straight. She'd have to straighten him out.

If things worked out the way MacAllister planned, Rock would soon be in Jail, charged with the murder of his friend, Stanley Norton, and Mary McCormick. Mac knew that Wesley Bjornquist was thinking along this same line of reasoning and would act the moment he got one small thing to use as evidence. Mac was sure he thought that Rock had killed Stan. She knew that if Rock were jailed, Kari would keep her promise. She would save Rock at any cost.

Now the question was, how was the going to get rid of Kari? If she'd only have had a chance to get at her before Bjornquist came. Obviously Kari had eluded Bengy.

Of course she must know that MacAllister couldn't let her run around free. Free to tell all she knew. Mac shivered.

There was nothing in evidence, in sight. No papers, no letters, nothing. Was it a letter? Or was it in some other form, something that only Rock would recognize? Mac began a systematic search.

Nothing escaped her searching fingers. And in the end, after every obvious and every remote place had been searched, MacAllister wondered if she were not overly concerned. Kari probably hadn't had time to write anything, much less hide it where it could not be found right away.

176

Perhaps she would find some way of telling Rock, some way to let him know who really killed his friend. The sneer at the corner of Mac's mouth deepened as she searched through the personal things in Kari's suitcases. An absolute peasant, she thought to herself. Why girls working in lesser jobs than Kari, had better lingerie than Kari's. Kari had few luxuries.

It was not in Kari's room. She may have put it in Rock's room before she went out thinking that he would find it right away, when he came from Bjornquist's office.

MacAllister moved methodically through Rock's room. Thorough, painstaking, until every possible hiding place hand been poked and prodded for the crackle of paper. On the desk, which she saved until last, was a pile of mail from the office. Rock had brought it home to sort and answer. The office. MacAllister had one brief moment of regret. She could not hope to hold the business. The business would be taken over by another law firm in Escanaba. One with whom Stanley had done a great deal of consultation. They had offered to take over the present calendar cases and she had told Rock to accept. She would have liked to keep an interest in the firm, but they were terse in their reasons why it was not possible. Strange, how she could look back at Stanley and their life together now, and be objective about it. He had only been a stepping stone to one of her goals. The goal of — first respectability, second — wealth, third — power. It was the last step on the ladder that had thrown her off balance. He had served his purpose. She had no qualms about removing him. It had been easy. It had been safe. Now there was no one to stand in her way. She would never have to fear the scorn and ridicule of being poor. She knew it had been difficult for many people to accept her into their clique, but it had been done because of Stan. Now they didn't dare shun her. She had too much on them.

As methodically as she did Rock's room, so all the rooms in the big house were examined. But in the end, after all the hiding places had been carefull checked, Mac abandoned the search.

As she was returning to the library from the second floor, she was conscious of a noise. It wasn't the noise of anything she could distinguish. It was like a sigh and a dull thud, muffled with wind and barks from the dog next door. Mac looked out across the huge lawn and into the other yard next door. She could see Bengy and Paul sitting on the porch with a huge dog snuggled between them. They were taking turns petting the huge animal.

Kari was there shooting arrows at a target. Effortlessly she pulled back the bow string, the arrow zoomed forward and buried itself with a loud thud in the red circle. Then Bengy took his turn with the bow and arrow. Kari and Bengy were talking between shots. MacAllister could see the serious look on Bengy's face and suspected that he might not be turning a deaf ear on Kari. She seemed to be arguing with him about something.

"I don't uderstand why you let Mac ruin your life, Bengy? Why don't you get out while you can?" she said.

"I can't. Did you ever do something which you knew was wrong? So wrong, that at night when you tried to sleep, it took complete coutrol of your mind and kept you awake?" Bengy paused a moment, arrow poised. "Why didn't you leave when Rock asked you to?"

"How did you know he told me to leave?" Kari asked

"I heard the conversation." Bengy let the arrow go and

it missed the target completely, digging itself into the wide area around the circle.

"There isn't much that goes on around here, that you don't know about, is there?"

"Not a great deal."

"Then, tell me this. Why did MacAllister kill Stanley?" She said this in so soft a voice that Paul, who was scramblin in the grass nearby with the dog, could not hear.

Bengy jumped. "Please! I wish you wouldn't talk like that. I can't sleep nights, I'm so full of it. I feel as guilty, as if I'd done it myself."

"But you were there, Bengy! Why did you let her do it?"

"I couldn't help it — it all happened so fast!"

"Why did you go away and leave him?" Kari persisted in her questioning.

"I don't know . . . I don't know!" he groaned and threw the bow on the grass, "God, if I only could go back and do it differently!"

"She must have a great hold of you, Bengy?"

"A hold? Yes, I guess it could be called that." He came closer to her. "Loving Mac is like a disease. It tears and pulls at your insides, until you are full of pain! But you can't fight it. It's like trying to rid yourself of your very soul. That's how I love Mac."

"I feel sorry for you." Kari picked up the bow and took the quiver from his shoulder. "I love Rock that much too, but I hope I'm never put to the test as you have been. I would probably do the same thing, then hate myself for the rest of my life."

"It's driving me crazy." Bengy sat down on the grass nearby.

"Why don't you tell Wesley Bjornquist?"

"I couldn't do that to Mac . . ."

"But what about Rock? Doesn't he matter, that an

179

innocent man is suspected of the murder? Don't you care
about this?"

"Not where Mac is concerned. I'm sorry Kari . . . believe
me, I am. But I'm as much to blame as Mac. I let her
do it. I could have phoned the doctor. I'm as guilty as she
is."

"Neither of them saw Mac until she was almost beside
them. She heard Bengy's last remark because she smiled
scornfully and said, "Yes. You had better be a coward,
Bengy, if you don't want to hang with me."

Both Kari and Bengy jumped, startled by her appearance. She had purposely chosen to approach from directly
behind them so she could get close enough to hear what
they were saying before they noticed her.

Paul heard her voice and got slowly to his feet, dog
forgotten. He edged toward the thick hedge and then
disappeared through it.

"Who's making the most points?" Mac asked, looking
at the target, then back at them.

Bengy said. "Kari, of course. You forget she's been
hunting deer in the northwoods for years."

"I didn't forget. I didn't know it."

"She's a deadly shot with that thing," Bengy added.
"Show her, Kari."

With almost a reflex action, Kari pulled an arrow and
aimed it at the target. With a whine and a dull thud it hit
the bull's eye. Automatically she pulled another and placed
in next to the other one. Three in a row. Then, realizing
that she had been shooting automatically she stopped
with a wry quirk at the corner of her lips.

"Ever shoot one?" she asked MacAllister.

"No. And I don't care to try."

"You'll stick to water and other things," Kari said, as

180

she pulled another arrow from the quiver and placed it smoothly along her left thumb. Her grip on the bow was strong without being tense. Firm without being tight. She spoke softly.

"I have seen many things in the northwoods. My father taught me to respect all living things. Animals as well as people. I have always lived by that rule. I have never killed an animal for the love of killing. Only when we needed food at the farm. I was taught that life is sacred and that no man shall kill another. Now I am beginning to wonder whether or not he was right. There are some people to whom life is not sacred. It is just a long visit on earth. Some stay longer than others. Usually there seems no real pattern to death. Now I wonder. I'm beginning to wonder whether some people wouldn't be better dead. What do you think Mac? Don't you think that some people need to be killed?" The left hand was slowly rising and the right hand grasped the string more firmly.

Kari looked straight into Mac's eyes with a detached stare.

"Put that damn thing down, Kari."

But Kari could not hear her words. She was not listening. The bow continued to lift slowly, surely as if she were in a trance. Her eyes had a far away look, the look of *a* hunter who has found his prey.

MacAllister stood without flinching. She watched the end of the arrow as it slowly lifted until it was pointed directly at her.

"Ask for mercy, Mac, plead for your life. Like Stanley did. Beg me, Mac."

"No. In the first place you couldn't do it, Kari, you're not the type. In the second place where would it get you? In jail with your precious fiance." Mac laughed in Kari's face. She turned her back and walked toward the house without another word.

Bengy stood horrified, and unable to speak as he watched the two women. He watched Kari hold the bow steady and point the arrow dead center on the middle of Mac's back. Slowly the string came back until the bend in the bow was almost maximum pull. He closed his eyes, his voice would not come past the restriction in his throat. He heard the bow's twang — then nothing.

He waited, eyes closed. He opened them slowly. At the last second before release, Kari's left had raised just before she let the arrow fly. It hit with a splat in the side of the house just under the old, unused observatory room near Paul's bedroom window.

# CHAPTER TWENTY ONE

As THE WHINE of the arrow passed directly over her head, Mac paused, then resumed her steady pace to the house. She didn't turn her head. She didn't look back. What Kari didn't know and couldn't see was the deathly white pallor that had spread over her face when she realized how close she had been to death.

Kari threw herself forward then, burying her head in the grass. Sobs wracked her body and the ground became wet with her tears. Bengy came over and knelt down beside her. Paul and the big dog came over to investigate. They had not seen what had happened. Only Bengy had seen.

He patted her shoulder gently. "Don't cry, Kari. Nothing happened. Thank God nothing happened."

Kari felt the dog's wet nose against the back of her neck, then a warm tongue as he, too, tried to console her. She could feel the soft hand of Paul, gently patting her head as he whispered, "Please don't cry! Please Kari."

It was a few minutes before Kari could control the flood of tears that tore her apart. She sat up and wiped at her face with Bengy's handkerchief. Paul, now that she had stopped crying, was romping with the dog over near the house. In a few minutes he disappeared from view and they could hear him yelling and the dog barking behind the house.

"I almost did it, Bengy," Kari finally said.

"I know. I thought you had. I couldn't look. I couldn't talk." His voice was still shaky.

"I should have. She's made life so miserable for so many."

"No, you shouldn't have. It's not for you to say who lives and who dies." Bengy shook his head sadly. "I only wish to God I had never seen Mac. She's like a disease, a malignant growth. She didn't use to be that way —" he closed his eyes as if to shut out the present and picture the past.

"I think she's lost her mind, Bengy. She can't be normal and do what she's done." She got slowly to her feet and started back toward the house. "I have to find Rock. I'm going to leave here right now. I can't stay in this house a moment longer."

"Get as far away as possible, Kari. Take Rock with you. Because," he paused a moment, "if you don't I'm afraid of what will happen." He matched his steps with hers.

MacAllister paused on the porch before she entered the house. The dog barked somewhere inside. Her legs were weak and she felt faint. She had turned her back on Kari thinking that she was only bluffing. When the arrow had passed over her head, she'd been too startled to duck and the swish of air had fanned her hair forward. The pause had been involuntary as she looked up. She'd wanted to run, but after the brief moment of fright she'd gone on.

Once inside she sagged against the door and a ragged breath escaped from her parted lips. That little bitch almost killed me, she thought. She hurried upstairs. There was something about the actions of Paul that she didn't like. Only this afternoon had she realized that Paul might have seen something the night of the murder. She had frightened him so the day after Stan's death, with her threats of punishment, that he'd never said anything. But the child had seen something. She could tell by the way he looked at her, then turned and ran. She'd tried to talk to him only this morning, but he'd given her a terrified look and ran from the house. She had not called him back. He wouldn't have come anyway she decided. She'd have to see what this was all about. As the arrow flashed overhead she'd looked up and had seen it bury itself in the wood under the observatory.

Strange she'd never given a thought to the old relic, hidden most of the year in the thick foliage of the huge oak tree. It had never occured to her that it was more than an eye sore, until now. She had never been interested in it. Just once — when she first married Stan — she'd asked what it was. He had explained that his grandfather, who had built this home, liked to watch navigation in the harbor.

As she was half way up the stairs she heard a door close. Paul must have come in the back way, she thought. She might as well find out right now, what he had seen.

When she reached Paul's bedroom she could hear noises from within. She knew Paul must have taken the dog upstairs with him. She'd heard him bark.

The door was unlocked and she pushed it open. The huge beast stood in the middle of the room looking at her. He neither wagged his tail or snarled but he faced her with a attitude as if he were standing his ground, protecting something, someone.

"Paul!" Her voice was soft, velvety.

She walked farther in the room and the big dog backde up only slightly, his eyes never leaving her face. It made her feel uncomfortable.

"Paul! Where are you? I know you're here so you might as well come out! Paul!" She stamped her foot and heard the low rumble of the huge dog as he stepped forward and stood stiff legged there before her.

"Lie down." she commanded. But the dog was not influenced by either her tone or her manner, certainly not because she was MacAllister Norton.

"Paul!" She was becoming more furious by the moment. "Come out here this instant and call off this damn dog." But still there was no answer.

It was then that she heard a rustle. She wasn't sure where it had come from but she walked past the dog and over to the window. He didn't move, just watched her. He obviously knew she wasn't afraid of him, at least he had done nothing to make her afraid. She heard the rustle again and then caught a flash of movement out of the corner of her eye. It came from the cupola. Through the dirty windows she could see the frightened face of Paul peering at her, trying to keep back out of sight, but also wanting to know what she was doing in his room.

She motioned to him to come in. But he stared at her, his eyes wide with fear. She remembered when Stan had showed her the cupola, long ago, that he had mentioned a small opening, just large enough for one person to

186

squeeze through. She walked slowly to approximately where the cupola was located and looked around for the door. It was so well concealed that only knowing where to run her hands along the elaborate moulding to find the small button latch, could she open the door. She pressed the button and saw the door slide open. She squeezed through the narrow space and stood inside the windowed cupola. She could see Bengy and Kari down on the lawn, over by the target, but Paul had again disappeared.

Then she saw him. He had opened the small window next to the house and slid out on the wide ledge that decorated the building. He seemed at ease, as though he'd been there many times before.

She leaned out and called to him, her voice lowered to a purr, the anger in it evident only to those who might hear. "Paul, come in this minute. You'll fall. Please, Paul, come here."

But Paul had already disappeared around the corner of the building. He was out of sight. He was on the side of the building that looked down into the "L" formed by the jutting library on the first floor.

She threw her slim leg over the sill and stepped out on the ledge, feeling as she did so, the breeze from the lake. A view of the entire grounds, front and back. Truely a lookout place.

Four careful, sliding steps took her to the corner of the biulding. Then she saw Paul. He was crouched down flat, his back against the house and his legs under him, fitted into the nook at the end of the ledge. Below her she could see directly into the library. This was a perfect vantage point for anything that transpired within.

Her eyes were slits of anger as she pictured the events of the evening Stan died. She knew now why Paul was

187

afraid. He had been out on the ledge, where he seemed quite at home — as if he'd spent many hours here.

"So you know." she said softly. She still was at the corner of the building. Behind her she didn't hear the rumble of the dog as. he stood, paws on the window sill, watching her. She only saw Paul, paralyzed with fear, huddled there against the house unable to move, unable to get away.

He nodded. "You killed him," he whispered, "I saw you — you killed him!" These were his first words to her since that night. Now these came rushing forth with hysteria behind them. He said them over and over as if he were unable to stop. She took another careful step and said, "Come in, Paul. You and I must talk. You are ill. You don't know what you're saying. Come in, Paul." she held out her hand to him.

This started the tears and he moaned with them, crying with huge, hurting sobs that came from deep inside. Sobs mixed with words. "You killed him — you killed him — you killed him —"

"You little fool —" he facc was contorted. It would only take a little push. There would be no one else who could tell. He was the only one. He was the only one she could not control. It would come out sometime. Just one little push. The tree would hide her movements. No one would ever know.

She edged slowly forward, the ground below seemed far away, she dared not look down. A wave of nausea passed over her and she hugged the building frantically for a moment, unable to move. She did not see the dog behind her as he watched her disappear around the corner. She did not see him balance uneasily first on the sill then on the ledge as he carefully lowered first one long leg, then the others in quick succession.

She did not see him as he walked slowly along, nose pointed down to the ledge, eyes forward, uneasily.

She didn't see him when he turned the corner. Neither she nor Paul noticed him until he snarled and rushed when she started to reach for Paul. She only was conscious of his huge body squeezing between her and the side of the house.

# CHAPTER TWENTY TWO

LATER, IN THE library, Bengy sat with head bowed and explained to Bjornquist, the world of MacAllister Norton.

Rock, with Kari, sat on the divan. Paul, after being rescued by the fire department from his place on the ledge, had been given a strong sedative and had been put to bed.

Mr. McTavish sprawled lazily at the foot of the bed, guarding his young master. The men had a difficult time getting the dog from his perch but finally had thrown a net over him and lowered him, squirming and indignant, to the ground.

"I was in talking to Wesley when the call came," he said to Kari. "I found the things I'd been looking for. Things which would have convicted Mac. She had lost Stan. She could only see one solution. She could never stand to lose what she'd taken so many chances to gain. It's better this way." His voice had sorrow in it, "the papers will be destroyed. There will be nothing for them to fear now."

"Them?" Kari wondered.

"People. Stan's friends. People who loved and respected Stan for years. Until he married Mac."

A week later, Kari and Rock stood on the observation platform of the "400" looking down at Paul and Signe on the platform below. Mr. McTavish, the mongrel, sat stoically beside Paul, looking around nonchalantly.

"Be a real good boy, Paul," Rock was saying, "and we will meet you in exactly two weeks. Take good care of him, Signe. It will be nicer for both of you to get away for a while. You'll like Milwaukee. And we we can straighten things out later." His arm was around Kari. He bent over and kissed her nose gently. "Button nose," he grinned, "we've got a wedding to attend and a honeymoon —"